I0690693

TIME TO MOW and OTHER SHORT STORIES

Zdravka Evtimova

TIME TO MOW and OTHER SHORT STORIES

Copyright © 2012 by Zdravka Evtimova

ISBN 13: 9780985778941

Library of Congress Control Number: 2012943572

Cover design by All Things That Matter Press
Published in 2012 by All Things That Matter Press

VASSIL

Vassil had decided to let himself go all the way. He had spent last night with a blonde, again, and had not even bothered to remember her name. She told him she had died and regenerated seven times and Vassil had pretended to believe her. But, the superficial black stripes on her shoulders and head, when you parted her hair, told a different story. Especially the ones on her head. They were so close together they gave him chills. She must have been in the regenerating rooms at least a dozen times, probably in the "deluxe" accommodations, the treatment followed by a lavish and costly procedure—the color of her skin summoned thoughts of fabulously expensive balm. Vassil had erased her face from his videotheque, but he was still in the throes of last night's excitement, so he decided to indulge himself with another blonde tonight. He knew that pleasures of this sort cost approximately three times his salary, but he was sure he would fail the physical exam this month and then would be forced into the standard regenerating rooms. The treatment left such deep and visible dark grey lines all over the body that afterwards one looked like a quilt sewn together from differently colored rags and bits of fabric. He considered himself born under a lucky star because the computer for initiating intimate contacts had paired him with such a charming creature: flaxen-haired, with green eyes that moved about in a distracted way, and an appearance that, at first glance, revealed no signs of her ever having set foot in a standard regenerating room. Impatient, Vassil wanted to proceed to the dark hotel room, for which he had paid a fat bundle, but when the woman said a few words he felt goose-bumps up and slowed his steps.

"You know, death looks quite becoming on you, dummy. Don't try to fight it! Don't try to hide the lines on your skin! They give a fierce expression to your face. You know, I sometimes envy those who go through the standard procedure."

Vassil hesitated. He could get rid of her—the woman was obviously crazy. But after a moment's thought he remembered that the computer for initiating intimate contacts had already charged him for the room, so he decided against it. The blonde woman had already started to caress him, and that switched on a pleasant sensation. Crazy or not, at least she does it well, he thought. Besides, I'll never see her again. Actually, the rules for intimate contacts did allow partners to meet repeatedly, but no one ever did. It would have been much too boring. The woman went on with her chatter.

"Just imagine, dummy. Sometimes I spend a whole six months without having to use the regenerating rooms"

Though he was generally regarded as a stable, well-composed person who could control himself, Vassil trembled visibly. This one was definitely off her rocker. Not that all the ones he had met before had been sane. Actually Seva, the only woman whose name he could remember and about whom he kept inquiring among his colleagues, was also mad. So mad, in fact, that he couldn't think about her without ending up dead drunk, thus using up his next two or three paychecks before he had even received them. Seva, an unusual name. When he had heard it for the first time he had made fun of it. He knew he would never see her again.

"Six months and not a single viral infection in my blood! No rheumatism, no diabetes, nothing. I'm completely healthy."

Vassil decided to ignore her rambling and babbling. He knew for a fact that it was impossible to survive on earth for more than a month without resorting to the regenerating rooms. The atmosphere was so filled with poisons and toxins that your lungs fell apart in forty days. Contact with the soil turned your skin into dust within a week. Water discolored and decomposed your blood in a month or so, provided you drank it in small doses. At least that's what he had been told. He ,himself, had never stayed away from the regenerating room for more than fifteen days.

"Six months without regeneration!" He grunted, trying to humor her. "Where do you work, honey?"

"At the Resurrection Laboratory," she chimed in. "Everything there is so sterile, so boring, that—"

Vassil whistled. "The Resurrection laboratory!" Some of the people who worked there could be quite refined, but sometimes they felt drawn to brutal, primitive characters, and put their numbers in a regular computer for initiating intimate contacts. But who cared? People got tired of always being among the elite. Vassil had chanced upon just such a woman. Maybe he could ask her. He was wary. Still, he could ask. It was too soon, though. Perhaps a little later. Vassil swore under his breath. The week after they dragged Seva away in a police van, he and two colleagues had tried to die permanently. Naturally, they had been regenerated once more and sent back to work. Society needed their golden hands, their invaluable experience; that's what the television commentator had said. Vassil had even received a pay-raise. Still, he had little tolerance for this society, this horde of dreary characters who had been regenerated a million times. Sometimes he wished he would never be resurrected again, would never have to go back to his dingy office and dreary job as a wholesale distributor of soap and cosmetics. But there was nothing he could do about it. It was much cheaper to regenerate the sickly and diseased and let them loose on the hazards of life fit and healthy than it was to purify the sludge-like soil or the brownish muck they called, by force of habit, water. The need to have children born had disappeared, and so had the need to squander money on hospitals, schools, kindergartens and nursery schools. People came back regenerated, their experience intact, their health fully restored, bragging about this disease or that which they had had earlier but had been cured, and so on until the next dying time. Women didn't lose their sexual savvy like this doll here. She was okay. Real death simply ceased to exist. And yet Vassil hated his job as a wholesale soap distributor with a passion.

"You know, dummy", blurted the blonde excitedly, "once they nearly threw me out of the Laboratory. Do you know why?"

"Why?" Vassil echoed listlessly.

"I absentmindedly left a patient's blood plasma out in the sun. You have no idea what happened to this man after we regenerated him! The poor idiot had a horn growing right out of his chest! He went berserk and gutted the chief surgeon, ripped open the faces of a couple of nurses. What excitement! Naturally, we had to regenerate all of them.'

Vassil felt himself getting tense. He licked his lips with a gravelly tongue. His blood pounded away in his temples.

"And what ever happened to that character, the one with the horn?"

"We had to liquidate him, of course," laughed the blonde.

"And then you ran him through the regenerators again?"

"Absolutely not! We liquidated him forever."

Vassil let out a groan. The blonde kissed him and resumed her benumbing prattle. But he was thinking of Seva, that mad woman. "I want a child" she had said to Vassil, "a real child. Mine and yours. I'll take care of it. Please, hide me somewhere. At your office" At first Vassil had said no. Then he thought, Why not? Then he took Seva to his squalid hole of a place. At least that way they wouldn't withhold money from his sex account until the police inspectors found her. And then the child was born. At first Vassil thought he would kill it; he had never heard of a child being born, and couldn't even start guessing what kind of fine they would impose on him for it. He had hidden Seva and taken her through the regenerating rooms illegally. This was going to cost him a fine of a quarter of a million! He had to get rid both of Seva and the baby. But he couldn't do it; from the moment the boy was born everything had changed. He would hurry like mad to get home. He would lean over his old clothes where the little one lay cuddled. He would pay outrageous sums of money for clean, filtered water. Eventually, however. the police found Seva. Vassil couldn't find out who had betrayed him; probably some friend who sincerely felt for him and wanted to spare him the disgrace and the huge fine.

"My colleagues will never believe me I ever came into contact with a person like you" said Vassil. The blonde laughed.

"Take this," she said, thrusting a bundle of cash into his hand. "Now they will believe you."

"The word was going around that you had regenerated some baby in your laboratory," Vassil ventured. The blonde tensed up nervously in his grasp, so he added quickly, "Maybe we shouldn't talk of such things?"

"No, we shouldn't," the woman smiled, calming down. "Apparently, some perverse character had wanted something stupid like that around. The woman with the baby refused to give his name."

Seva! It dawned on him like a huge submarine suddenly emerging from the depths of the ocean. Seva. She had not betrayed him. Of course she hadn't. If she had told on him they would have sent him to Seycard. There, the regenerating rooms were set up so that when you came out your eyes popped out and glazed over, and you went mute. But there is a use for idiots; doctors have to have material to experiment on. So Seva had not betrayed him. Mad, stark raving mad. She could have accused

4

him of rape and coercion, but she hadn't. He had promised his annual salary as a reward for any information on her. Maybe someone had run into her in some intimate contact. But no one had ever responded. He was going crazy with fear that they had sent her to Seycard, so he signed on as a volunteer to go and repair the facilities there, but he didn't find her. The thought of her being with someone else drove him insane with jealousy. But at least that was preferable to knowing with certainty that they had not regenerated her, that she had disappeared from the face of the earth. "Seva. My dear—"

"What?" the blonde shrieked in delight. "My dear? Is that what you just called me? You're incredible sweetie."

"Dear?" Where had he picked up the word? No one had used it in years. Seva. Seva. Seva ...."Did you really regenerate that baby?" Vassil threw in gingerly.

"Why in the world would we do that? No, we left it to its own end."

"To its end? To ... die?" he froze with fear at the sound of the word. "To die forever?"

"Of course, dummy." The blonde woman smiled and started stroking his hair. "Both the baby and his hare-brained mother, who, come to think of it, wasn't bad looking at all. Will anybody believe that you called me "My dear"? I really liked it, though it did sound kind of loony, didn't it?"

If only he had tried to stop the paramedics when they took the baby away! Vassil hadn't shown his face at all. That would have meant regeneration at Seycard for sure. He remembered how the day before he had taken the little one's fingers and put them to his own cheek. Loony, true, but nice. It had felt so nice! Somehow he had hoped that at some point in his life he would see a boy and say, "That's my boy." He had hoped ... but they would see! He would show them! Maybe it would have been better if Seva had betrayed him back then.

"They'll see, all of them!" he kept repeating after the blonde beauty had departed. His joints hurt, his heart had been rattling irregularly for quite some time. He was definitely due for another regeneration. As usual, Vassil carefully prepared his blood plasma. But this time, contrary to all instructions, he left the transparent container out in the sun for more than an hour. "They'll see, Seva!" Vassil hated his job at the soap office more than ever before.

His first impulse when he emerged from the next dying and regeneration routine was to reach out and feel his chest. "Seva, my dear!" he whispered. Those forgotten, silly words. In the middle of his chest cavity his shaking fingers touched a crusty, sharp-edged protrusion.

It was a huge, heavy horn.

They didn't know!

A PILLOW FOR ITALY AND SPAIN

Winter was wild this year. The sky was full of snow and wind; the trees in front of the cafe looked like stubbly old men in the white air; and, it was cold in the narrow room overlooking the Struma River that flowed tiredly, grumbling to its rocks. Gogo slept by her side, bent double, his skin whiter than the January sky. She lived in the café, in the back room overlooking the river. She liked the guys who serviced the big truck that collected the garbage on Main Street. They drank her coffee, their black eyes pushing under her old blue apron.

"I'll buy you a silver ring," the shortest of them said once, but Viah knew he didn't have money; none of the guys had money. Yet they looked at her as if they could buy her the sky, and the small park covered with dirty snow. She had rented the cafe and had named it 'Viah Cafe' after herself. It was the favorite haunt of the men who collected the garbage, the men from the slate quarry and from the slaughterhouse. They all brought their smells with them—slaughtered animals, gunpowder, occasionally garbage—and they brought their eyes, too.

She always had someone, the strongest one, the man who had slaughtered the most animals. Now the man who had killed the most barren cows slept by her side with his white skin that sparkled by her brown body. He held her in his dreams. That man's name was Gogo, but the guys called him Blood. His nose had been broken several times.

In the afternoons, he stopped her in the cafe to sniff her blue apron. "You smell sweet," he said, but that could hardly be true. Cigarette smoke crept up to the ceiling and the room was thick with suspicious odors of boots, wet coats, and the aroma of the soup boiling on the cooking stove. The men watched him smell the collar of her apron and didn't dare to utter a sound, their eyes buying Viah every drop of the Struma River—from its source to the Aegean Sea. Whenever Gogo showed up in the cafe, whether it be at noon, daybreak, or at 2 a.m., Viah went right away to that cold bed in the backroom which was full of vodka and big demijohns of brandy. She loved him till she left him perfectly mousy and powerless in his unbelievably white skin.

"I'll buy you a gold bracelet" he whispered choking, but Viah knew he was broke. Blood gave her all his money and she bought cheap brandy for the men who drank it in the cafe. She preferred not to think of the bad brandy while she listened to his happy voice that lied to her about the bracelet. Even at noon, when the men who collected the garbage ordered French fries, Gogo, glowing like an ember, waited for her in the backroom. She came in and stayed until his skin could no longer love her. Several times the French fries turned into coals in the pan. The dustmen learned to take chicken livers out of the fridge, then fried and ate them underdone as they listened to the sounds coming from Viah's backroom.

"Come with me to Italy," Gogo asked her once. He had made arrangements to go to Calabria. There were so many olive trees there, you picked olives all day and the Italians, who were frog-eaters as he had heard, paid you handsomely. But how could he go to Calabria when Viah waited for him in the cafe? He didn't get into fights any more, for if he got slashed he would have to go to the hospital, and that would mean he'd lose a precious day with her.

"Won't you start for Italy?" She asked him one day. "You'll miss the season of olives."

He simply could not go; she was like food for him. He'd be starving without her. Viah looked thoughtfully at his white skin, at his face that was a most ordinary stubbly face. She had watched another white face before his, an almost beardless face of another man, who slept at exactly the same place in the bed by the wall. That was Radomir, the only son of the old man who made the wild fruit brandy.

"You have to leave for Calabria tomorrow," she urged Gogo. He woke up, said to her 'come on' and she did, giving him what he wanted. Then she repeated, "You have to leave for Italy tomorrow."

She thought of the brandy in the big demijohns. Or rather, she thought of the old man who brought the brandy. He was Radomir's father. Radomir picked olives in Spain. In the evening he often called her on her mobile. He told her he counted the days that separated him from her and her narrow room. He was the brandy man. His father brewed the brandy, allegedly out of plums, but what plums could anyone brag about when the trees in his orchard had withered a long time ago?

The old man put various things into the brandy, simmered it gently for hours, mixed sloes, haws and damsons, and perhaps he cursed it a lot, for his concoction tasted like death. The geezer moved quietly like a grass snake; he crawled up and down the hills of Barren Ridge for miles and miles to find a damson tree. The sun had baked his skin, winds from Greece scorched him and rains from Macedonia drenched him. He dragged an enormous sack into which he thrust wild pears, damsons, rose-hips for his brandy, thinking how he'd bring it to Viah. He came early in the day, twice a week, silent like soot, and she recognized him by the smell of wild fruits and berries. She liked that smell.

She said she liked the old man's brown woolen jacket in which he dressed himself up for her. Viah didn't mind that he had tried to kill the odor of rotten pears by pouring a bucketful of cheap cologne over his face and hands.

She kissed him gently. She did not leave him alone until his thin face glowed with happiness. Viah kissed him, ignoring the brand new shirt he had put on especially for her. She did not think about the enormous demijohns of brandy he made out of cornels and haws. She admired him. She truly respected him. He did so well for his age.

Afterwards, she gently took him out of the narrow room and asked him to get into his old boneshaker. There the old man slept, his head propped against the rusty steering wheel, his woolen jacket thrown over his shoulders to keep him warm. Viah always wrapped him up, left a bottle of wild brandy for him and thrust a loaf of bread into his paper bag.

Then, the place next to the wall in her bed was free for Gogo.

"You have to leave for Calabria, yes you have to. There are heaps of olives to pick there. The biggest olives in the world grow in Calabria. Go there quick, or other guys will pluck them all."

"You come with me and I'll start packing right away," Gogo said.

"Come off it," Viah answered absentmindedly, thinking of Radomir. He was soon to return from Spain. He called her in the dead of night to tell her that the raindrops were as big as walnuts, that the winds smelled of her and reached into his very bowels. He said it felt nasty in Spain because Viah was not there. The Spanish women were so short and squat. Night in, night out, Radomir told Viah he felt she was close to him. Viah

9

listened to what he was going to do to her when he came back and smiled at the demijohns. He asked her if his father brought her wild berry brandy twice a week, as they had agreed, and wanted to know whether the jerks from the slaughterhouse annoyed her.

"Everything is Okay," Viah answered. "Yes, yes." She was waiting for him. She had even bought a new pillowcase for his pillow, which waited for him, too. He had to stay a little more in Spain, though.

All the electrons in the air gathered in Radomir's voice and shouted that Viah was the greatest Spanish woman he knew, the tallest and the prettiest Spanish woman, although she was Bulgarian, every single inch of her. The girls he happened to meet in Spain were fools. Then he promised miserably he'd endure one more week in the Spanish rain, thinking of his new and clean pillowcase. All right, Viah answered him as she served the unshaven garbage collectors their brandies and sensed their eyes on her blouse. Stay in Spain one week more, she thought to herself.

"You have to leave for Italy," she told Gogo softly. He had gathered himself up and asked her to join him again, and she was about to, but then she suddenly thought she could not accommodate both Spain and Italy on the same clean pillowcase. She was sure that the season of the olives could not go on forever. She often thought of the old men, too. She could not tell him every time that on the following Thursday they'd get into his boneshaker and spend the night on Barren Ridge under stars as tiny as dust.

She loved Radomir, she loved Gogo and she loved the old wild brandy man.

Sometimes she thought she should leave the cafe and say good bye to the men who collected the garbage. She could rent another cafe, a little warm hole, far away from the Struma River, from the bearded snowy willows, the dark eyes that she liked better than any brandy under the sun. She'd sure find another cheap backwoods cafe. Maybe the whole country was a warm, cheap cafe; maybe she, too, was the only warm cafe for men who were to leave for Spain to pick olives or make houses for the Spanish women. She knew she should go away, but she loved Radomir, she loved Gogo, and she loved the old wild brandy man so much.

WRONG

The smell was there again and I turned around. It was sweet and it made me smile, and I wondered where it came from. There was no one in sight, the street stretched before me, endless and gray, the buildings were gray, too; the sky looked heavy with lightning, but the smell was there. There was no doubt about that. Then I noticed the car—a most ordinary gray Ford. I suddenly remembered I saw it yesterday when I went to work, and I remembered the smell was there, too. I approached the car, curious and a little frightened. A gray-haired man sat in it.

"Can I help you, Ma'am?" the man asked. I looked at him closely. It turned out his hair was brown, not gray.

"I remember your car," I said. "I think I noticed it yesterday."

"Yesterday?" the man said pursing his lips. "It's impossible, Ma'am. I wasn't in that town yesterday."

I thought one could hardly dub "town" the dozen of ramshackle houses and the narrow asphalt road that touched the apathetic buildings and climbed to the black sky in the distance.

"Your car smells sweet," I said. "I noticed that yesterday."

The man was silent, staring at the windshield, his sharp profile a slab of white marble cutting the gray air. He seemed to have forgotten all about me. What the hell, I said to myself. My ex-boyfriend used to behave in exactly the same way—he stared at the night and forgot all about me. He didn't even notice when I went out. Men tended to forget me very quickly, I had noticed that a number of times. I think it had to do with my constant talking. What the hell, I left the guy in his sweet smelling car and hurried along the street. My office was a block away. It was a hole of a room with a window next to a clump of poplar trees that made me allergic almost half of the year. I didn't know what I hated most: my constant allergies, the translations I did ten hours a day, or the thought of my boyfriends who seldom noticed I was there.

I remembered the boring novella I had to translate by the end of the week and shuddered—it was a story about a banal love affair. The word 'love' gave me the creeps. It reminded me of my latest boyfriend who said he had had enough of my whims and vagaries. Well, I worked hard and I made efforts to understand if the protagonist hated the world in general, or only his cheating wife and her lover. In my opinion the protagonist was a particularly unintelligent fellow. He delivered long monologues teeming with Latin quotations on the future of the world. I could not stand the guy and his ideas of the future. I thought my ex-boyfriend looked very much him—boring and moralizing.

Then once again the sweet smell was there, it was in my nose. The gray car ground to a halt and the man in it said, "I could give you a lift to your office."

"How come you know where I work?" I asked suspiciously.

"I'm the author of the novella you are translating," the man said.

"Oh."

"Your boss said you didn't like my work," the author of the damned thing said.

"No, I don't like it," I said. There was no use pretending. The novella was no good, and its author looked like my ex-boyfriend.

The minute I said this I knew I had made a serious mistake. I suspected the guy might withdraw his writings and assign the translation to my colleague. She was more amiable than me; she admired the dirges she translated, called the authors geniuses and their prose concoctions were all masterpieces to her. Malomed, that's how that woman's name was, made twice more money than me. She had a poet boyfriend she called Dante instead of Don. His poetry gave me headaches.

"Why does his poetry give you headaches?" the author asked.

"What!" I must have been thinking aloud.

I did think about Don's doggerels, but I was positive I hadn't said anything about them. I was short of money and I wanted the translation of that novella and that was what interested me.

"I'll give you a lift to your office," he said.

When I got into the car he said, "Why don't you like my work?"

"It's not so much I don't like it …." I knew how I needed the money. The orange ford ground to a halt once again.

"You lied to me," the guy said. "That's why the car stopped."

"Oh, come off it," I said. "I lie to many people every day, but my car doesn't stop on account of that."

12

"I don't lie to people," the man said, looking at me in a way that suddenly made me angry. I felt like shouting at him —which I did.

"Your prose is no good," I said. "It gives me the creeps."

The minute I stopped talking I noticed the car didn't move at all. The stranger had killed the motor.

"What are you waiting for?" I told him. "I'll be late for work and my boss will give me a piece of her mind."

"It's not my fault," the man said. "The car moves only when the passenger is happy."

I thought about it. I wasn't happy at all. I thought I didn't have a single happy day in my life.

"Try to think about the time when you loved your boyfriend," the author of the boring novella said.

"I didn't love my boyfriend," I said. "He dumped me so quickly and I didn't have the chance to even start loving him."

It was raining outside, and the gray sky touched the windshield of the car. It was quite dark and the clouds looked as thick as the asphalt. The car suddenly skidded forward.

"I am not happy at all," I said to the driver. "Why did the car move?"

"I was happy," the man said. "I think I like you."

I studied the man's face. I wouldn't say it was attractive, just an ordinary man's face the type I wouldn't bother to look at twice. It was raining and I was angry.

"Look here," I said. "You thought up the whole thing, didn't you?"

"I thought up what?" he asked.

"The automobile thing. You're lying to me. You stop the car and you make it go whenever it suits you."

"I didn't think anything up. What I've told you about the car is true. I like you and the car moves forward."

"Then your car must stop right away, because I can't say I like you," I said bluntly. Then I noticed I held an ashtray in my hands. I had taken it from the panel in front of me. It was an ugly thing, yet most unexpectedly it smelled sweet, too.

"Are you a smoker?" I asked the man. "I hate smokers, let me tell you that."

The sweet smelling car stopped. It rained harder, the clouds turning the street into a lake of churning water. The driver bristled up.

"Are you sure you don't like me?" he asked.

"I am," I answered.

First the sweet smell vanished, then suddenly I was in the middle of a puddle in the street. There was no car, and no man by my side. Now that's bad, I said to myself. I'm hearing voices and I'm seeing things. My latest boyfriend had warned me I'd be out of my mind in no time at all; he said no one could stand me, so evidently I was starting to invent a man who could put up with all my tricks. My shoes were dripping wet, my hair and my clothes were an avalanche of cold shivers crawling down my spine. My fingers were cold, too. I thought I'd better rub them to get warm when I noticed I still held the ashtray in my hands: an ugly thing that held the sweet smell of the car which had vanished in the rain. "Hey!" I shouted. "Where are you?"

There was no one in the street, and I was completely sodden, shivering with cold. My boss glared at me the minute I entered the office.

"Your deadline is 30th March," she said. "I want the translation of the first 15 pages now."

I didn't have the fifteen pages ready.

"I am afraid it would be impossible, Mrs. Whitaker," I said feeling her eyes bite me. "I have a rough draft of the translation and I need time to polish it."

The azaleas in the street blossomed palely in the rain. There was cold rain in Mrs. Whitaker's eyes, too. I wanted to go on a short holiday to Ostende, at the Nord Sea. I had been there once and the wind was so strong I could lie on it. The sea was the color of asphalt and there were no people along the beach. I had listened to the waves for hours, and ate a pizza in the Neapolitana Café.

"By the way, there's a letter for you," Mrs. Whitaker grumbled. Everyone knew how much she disliked forwarding messages to her employees. "I'm not a post office, mind you," she reminded me as she chucked the envelope onto my desk.

It was the only letter I had received for years. I mean an ordinary letter, one typed on a sheet of paper. It said "Neapolitana Café, 7 pm, today". There was all there was to it. I put it in my desk drawer. I thought

I could talk to that letter, or to the drawer in which I kept it, which didn't make much difference.

"By the way," Mrs. Whitaker said smiling. Her smiles were a bad sign. Her tall body leaned forward, her eyes hard. "I intended to assign the translation of the novella to Miss Malomed."

This didn't come as a surprise. Miss. Malomed, my amiable colleague, stated all pieces of fiction she happened to translate were masterpieces. The authors were always happy to meet her. They were not happy to meet me.

I looked at Mrs. Whitaker imagining the empty cold kitchen in my apartment and the heap of bills I still hadn't paid. I saw the heap of shirts and jackets which belonged to my ex-boyfriend. I still hadn't thrown them in the dust bin. Sometimes in the evenings, instead of translating, I gave his dirty shirts a piece of my mind. It did me good.

I imagined I could go to Ostenede again. I didn't remember the name of the wine I had drunk there.

"Well, I won't assign the translation to Miss Malomed," my boss went on, pausing significantly, watching my face.

***

When I woke in that shabby hotel room in Ostenede I found I didn't have enough money for a good breakfast. It was a rainy spring day, and there was no wind to listen to.

"The author of the novella phoned today," my boss made another of her important pauses, her upper lip a threatening piece of ice. Her face usually froze when she had a bad news to break. As a rule, her news was bad. She started by pointing out she had heard me talk to a handkerchief. That was true. It was my ex-boyfriend's handkerchief. I was telling it I was a pretty woman. I had spoken to the handkerchief using rare, morally offensive words in Bulgarian I was sure no one understood. My ex-boyfriend never did, so saying long nasty words to his shirts gave me exactly the same pleasure as if he was listening to me.

I missed the fragrance of the strange car, though. I missed the man's voice who had said he liked me.

I missed the intimate contacts with a boyfriend.

"The author of the novella said he liked your translation," my boss declared, the words dropping from her lips in a dead heap in front of me.

"I knew he would," I said, although I had not started translating the thing yet. It had been the most disappointing piece of writing I had come across for five years and two ex-boy friends.

"By the way, you know I disapprove of negotiations between the authors and my translators," Mrs. Whitaker croaked.

"I know," I said.

"I strongly disapprove my translators' talking to inanimate objects," she went on.

"I talk to objects to concentrate," I explained.

It rained hard outside.

"I wouldn't like to know anything about anybody's personal life, but …" she said.

I didn't tell her I had no personal life, barring my long conversations with my ex-boyfriend's shirts. My getting drunk alone in the Neapolitana Café couldn't qualify as personal life, either.

"That author said he'd like to give you a new part of the novella he had just written. That's the part that seems wrong," my boss said at last.

"Why should it?" I asked.

"You wouldn't want to know," her voice stretched too thin to cover all nuances of sarcasm and contempt she felt for me at the moment.

I'd have given two years of my life if only I could bark one of my morally offensive Bulgarian words in her face. Then there was that Malomed person, my colleague, enthusiastic and ready to oblige.

"In fact I told the boss I would be there for you. I mean, I could translate the damned piece if you," she chirruped. "I mean if you turned it down. Ms Whitaker thought you'd positively turn it down so—"

"I'll do it," I told her. She stared, her smile slowly sinking into her good shining teeth.

"O, I understand."

It was not too clear what she understood.

Then it was there again, the pleasant aroma that I liked so much, the fragrance of the grey automobile. I looked through the window and I didn't see the car. A minute later I caught a glimpse of the man who owned it, the writer of poor novellas. He was shaking Mrs. Whitaker's hand. I had not noticed when he'd entered the office. The man looked good, I had to admit that.

"It's there again, that smell," I told him.

"That smell?" he asked.

"Of the automobile," I answered. My boss stared at me. Malomed heaved another of her deep meaningful sighs.

"I can give you a ride to Neapolitana café," the writer of poor novellas said quickly.

The town was full of rain and azalea blossoms that made me horribly allergic. The car was there, though, in the street in front of our office, the sweet smelling automobile.

"Your colleague ... Miss Malomed," the author whose work I was translating said after we got into the car.

"Yes?" I muttered. I had a gut feeling the turn our conversation took would be no good. "I think we are wasting time."

"The car moves only when the passengers are happy," the man said. "I've told you that." He took a deep breath. "I think you are a good translator, but ... Maybe Miss Malomed—"

"You can go ahead and talk to Miss Malomed," I snapped. There was no point in going to Neapolitana café now, was there? The car had remained immobile in front of my office window, the azalea tree heaping its blooms in the wind just to exacerbate my allergy.

"Miss Malomed is a fine lady," the man started. I was reaching to open the door when he said in Bulgarian. "I don't care for Miss Malomed. I want you. I came here to see you. You are all I've been dreaming about."

I could not believe what I heard.

"You are everything to me. You are the air I breathe in, you are the wind I listen to, you are my happy evening and you are in all my words. Please, please don't go."

Suddenly I felt the sweet smelling automobile was moving. It was racing along the sleepy street of the town, it was hurtling and buzzing and singing and shouting with joy.

"You speak Bulgarian!" the man whispered. "You understood!"

"I am Bulgarian," I said.

Then I was suspicious. Was that another man who played with me, another mean trick? And I was stupid to rise to the bait. I was the dumbest thing in town. The car was about to grind to a halt.

"But it is true!" the man shouted in English. "I mean every word of it."

The car roared and rushed forward stronger and swifter than the waves in Ostende, a cloud of fragrance trailing in its wake.

"Who are you?" I asked amazed.

"I am the man who likes Bulgarian language," he said.

I believed what he said. He was the man I had been dreaming about all my life.

***

I was wrong one more time.

He didn't like Bulgarian language. He spoke Bulgarian only when he was happy.

GOLDEN CHIFFON AND VIOLONCELLO

It was the hottest day in Aachen, Nordrhein Westfalen Province since 1967, the meteorologists said on the radio. The air smelled of linden blossoms, of grass and warm winds from Belgium.

They went on doing it, my mother and Aunt Hedda, after whom I had been named. Both of them were dressed in long robes of golden chiffon that looked almost entirely new, although they had been putting on these dresses for seventeen years. They did it every evening. My mother played the violin, Aunt Hedda the violoncello.

Those were our happy nights when nobody but Mozart and Schubert existed; I was empty translucent space and the music was our common umbilical cord. Every evening the three of us were born again and again, beautiful, ethereal like cosmic darkness, or the radiance of a supernova. There the wrinkles on their faces and hands were invisible. They had not put on any weight and had not turned into formless bags of flesh. In spite of the years that had tried to ruin them, they sparkled with their golden chiffons, and the universe flew through their hearts slowly permeating my own, which was a very ordinary unmusical heart. I was the only daughter in our family of three. My mother and Aunt Hedda were sisters and if they didn't dye their hair it would be perfectly white; both of them were incredibly pretty, turning heads even when they had not put on their make-up.

Years ago, at the time when they were wearing their golden chiffon dresses, they had so many adorers, "crowds of passionate young men, my dear," as Aunt Hedda would put it. And, of course, they were flighty young girls. The gentlemen were so handsome and rushed in and out of their lives so rapidly that when, in the long run, the two of them landed each carrying a baby, almost at one and the same time, you could imagine the horror my late grandfather, a renowned concert violinist, lived through.

My late grandmother had panicked. Even on her deathbed, she was head over ears in love with her grey-haired husband who suffered from most of the diseases in the world. Grandmother had carried his picture close to her heart. Whenever she was in a lot of pain she pressed it to her skin, uttering his name, her lips livid, making efforts to overcome the fit, and he sat by her side holding her hand and trying hard not to cry before her. He had desperately wanted to convince her she'd be all right, and that they would live so many more days together in this wrong and bad world.

So when my mother and Aunt Hedda told their poor parents they were pregnant, but didn't know who the fathers of their babies were, my grandmother started shuddering and the tremor of fear remained in her fingers. She had surely lived through a crisis and had certainly collapsed into an abyss of inward despair because the poor soul had neither known nor loved another man but her beautiful violin player. My grandfather had been her moon and her native planet, her blood, her diseases and her failing health. All that was my grandfather to her, God bless his soul.

Awe struck, I touched his violin, which my mother played only when she was in love. I, the most unmusical, a figuratively deaf and inefficient member of our family, caught the dazzling light of music and stood immobile, transfixed with shock, staring at my mother as if she had flown to our house from another galaxy; as if she was not the woman who gave me money to buy chocolates and books, as if she was not the enraged she-wolf who constantly lectured me, ordering me to go out with my friends or have sex like the other girls in the neighborhood. Why should I rot with the books which filled my not-too-clever head with absurd stuff and lies about life? Why should I look at my feet while passing by clusters of young men? That was an absolute disgrace for the dead bones and blood of all the women of her family who had lived centuries before her.

I didn't see the narrow street I lived in, the pretty neat houses, the small lake Blaustein, and I didn't feel the winds coming from the Nord See whispering about sandy secrets, of hot dunes and loneliness.

When Mother played my grandfather's violin her eyes were humbly glued to the ground; she was in love with a worthy and wonderful man. Both Mother and Aunt Hedda had many men and few among them were wonderful. Judging by the shoes the men left on the threshold of my mother and Aunt Hedda's rooms, they were mostly pretentious big shots. My favorites were the shoes that had not been polished meticulously. In such cases I thought there was hope the boyfriends might be some normal ordinary guys.

Mother and Aunt Hedda were very beautiful; their blue eyes as deep and hot as the earth's core, their tall exquisite bodies remaining slim in spite of the huge amounts of *apfelstrudel* they constantly ate. They were convinced they killed their excessive weight through sex, but in my opinion, it was their blind absurd adoration of music that abolished the unwholesome substances in their blood. Mozart and Schubert were stronger than the poisons in the human body.

The black universe turned into white nebula in the strings of their instruments, chasing away the nasty men who sometimes left their perfectly polished shoes on the threshold of their rooms. Their music erased the dirty words that Aunt Hedda shouted at times in my presence, to teach me in advance how disgusting life was.

To cut a long story short, when Mother and Aunt Hedda told the violinist and his wife they were both expecting babies in July, the violinist said, "Das is nicht gefahrlich, girls, in other words, There's nothing to be afraid of. Go ahead. I hope I'll be strong enough to make money to feed two additional throats." As my late grandmother heard his calm tone of voice, in spite of the fact that the tremor of fear never left her arthritic fingers, she agreed there could be enough old dresses to cut into pieces and make swaddling clothes for two tots.

Aunt Hedda aborted her pregnancy because at that time she fell in love with a naval officer, a great charmer. My mother gave birth to me, a half smothered suckling, looking very blue in the face. The evening concerts of my mother and Aunt Hedda started with my first birthday, which they celebrated when I was five. And that was perfectly normal for two heavenly women who didn't care about anybody but Mozart and Schubert and about their concerts in the warm darkness. Unfortunately, my grandmother and grandfather died one after the other, the violinist outliving his beloved wife by eight days. We found him dead holding his instrument, which my mother played only when she was truly in love, as I have already said.

So no one taught me to play the violin or violoncello. I could only whistle different tunes. Mother and Aunt Hedda were with their handsome adorers whose perfectly polished shoes made me sick. I whistled the tunes I had heard at their dark concerts and fell asleep dreaming about Mozart. He composed another of his beautiful symphonies and I prayed I could hear it on the following day.

I could not love the town of Aachen and Blaustein Lake if I did not love my mother's and Hedda's music. It was in linden blossoms, in the rumble of the summer storms, in the windows of the clean houses that glowed at night. The concerts of Mother and Hedda were the happiest time in my life until I met one of my mother's men. He played the violin as well. Thin, fair-haired, very pale, so in the beginning I thought something had gone wrong with him. His face looked transparent. I even told mother not to have him in her room for he probably suffered from some serious disease. But he proved to be a very nice guy. His name was Konrad.

While Mother and Hedda entertained their boyfriends I listened to Konrad play his violin. I didn't know who the composers of his music were. It was neither a black universe nor a spring meadow. It was music of a tortured and ill man who probably saw death waiting for him among the semibreves and quarter notes. Perhaps he saw the world beyond he was to fly to after he left my room, or caught something in the air as he pushed aside the plate on which I had put a piece of stale cake for him, given as a present to Aunt Hedda by some of her numerous admirers. She had a sweet tooth and they brought her bars of chocolate and sweets.

I thought one never lied when he faced death. Konrad's music was quiet like the last drops of rain against the window, like hope that a guy would have enough time to eat the last crumb of the stale cake on his plate. His tune told death, "Wait. Let the girl listen to the last part of the piece. She likes it so much. It is not a black universe. It's not a spring meadow. It is not even a kiss. It's not pain. Let the girl listen on. I'll come with you when my piece is finished."

When I told Mother and Aunt Hedda I was expecting a baby they froze in their tracks, then screamed they were going to shoot dead all their boyfriends. They suspected one of them was to blame for my misfortune. It was Aunt Hedda who declared that we'd have enough money to feed a small thing like a child. Why should we be afraid of a baby, she asked? It's just some disposable nappies and milk bottles. Go ahead.

But when they learned I wanted to marry Konrad, they went through the roof. How was it possible? They both were very intelligent and gentle, but *nobody* got married these days, for Christ's sake! "All men are mean dogs, my dearest. He'll break your heart. He'll cheat on you and you will suffer. You know us very well, dearest. And we know men very well. They are nasty." Mother said Konrad might die soon and that was all right with her; I'd be free again and the three of us would bring up the child. Let's hope it would be a girl. They didn't let Konrad enter our apartment, saying there was no place for such a wretch in our family.

Once, they heard him play the violin in the street at the entrance of our house. He was playing not for death, but to his daughter who was not born yet. Some time after that Aunt Hedda said, "Listen to me. There may be place for him in our sitting room. What do you say?" And that was so much from a woman who had been playing the violoncello for twenty-one years now, had been dreaming of dark men, of the child she had not given birth to, and of the naval officer who had broken her heart. Now she was going to have a granddaughter, and if God didn't call her in to heaven to play her violoncello for him then my baby would be a great violist. Her blue eyes had said as much and they never lied.

Konrad told me that a river of stars flowed in the strings of his violin after he met me. He said he was happy I lived in that narrow street in Aachen. I thought he was my native planet, my disease and my health, and I swore that I'd ask Aunt Hedda to play something for him when she fell in love with someone. At such moments her eyes sparkled. They were the most beautiful eyes anyone could ever have.

I'M HOME

Keith knew Hilda would understand. She always did. She was the perfect wife. He sat by the window and she knew she didn't have to make the slightest noise. If he sat by the fireplace she knew she had to bring him coffee, he liked his coffee black and she remembered that well. She was a woman of little words; he felt at home in her silences. She felt comfortable like an old pair of slippers. And, she didn't meddle with his collections.

He had married her after she dropped out of college. He learned she wrote poetry. He read a couple of her poems and told her he didn't think much of them.

He had three hundred and eleven miniature elephants of marble and ebony, of mahogany and silver, malachite and gold. Hilda had never been inquisitive and that was a thing about her he liked. She helped him with his research and she chose the exquisite vases of different forms, which Keith admired so much. He had a passion for collecting ancient furniture and books, and his house was a treasure of collectibles. Not a single item in it was ordinary or cheap. Keith could truly breathe only in his spacious study, which Hilda kept in perfect order. She took care of all: his miniature elephants, the golden and silver coins, the rugs, each one a treasure, and the seven halls full of books, which she had arranged neatly in alphabetical order of their authors.

He had a ritual. In the evenings, he sat in his study a glass of Chablis in hand, and rang his ancient Belgian silver bell. She brought him a tome of the "History of the Roman Empire" and read to him. Her soft voice, the smell of the leather binding and that peculiar aroma of quiet dust calmed him down.

She read beautifully.

***

She always knew when he had another woman.

Keith couldn't tell how on earth she deciphered this. Perhaps he ignored the TV, or perhaps he became too talkative. She knew, but she didn't ask who the woman was. She understood. Keith was a collector. He collected memories of enjoyable days with women. All the women were expensive and perfect like the objects in his house. Funny, he missed Hilda when he was out, happy with a new conquest.

At times he wished Hilda chose the women for him. She had perfect taste. She never asked where Keith was and why he didn't come home on time. Her reticent silence waited for him. His house met him brilliantly clean; his miniature treasures sparkled, arranged in perfect rows with tags, reminding him of where and at what price he had bought the object. His golden coins were there for him and his bed offered him good rest. But above all this clean and efficient smiling and acquiescing Hilda waited for him.

He had given her a lifetime of peace and security. She was a barmaid before she met him. Her skin was older than that of the girls he had been happy with. There were lines at the corners of her mouth. Keith welcomed them. She was growing old more quickly than him and that fact was quite reassuring. She was like the rain in Brussels of which he had become accustomed: cold and clean. He loved it when she cooked for him. She didn't talk, nor, look at him, but concentrated on the ingredients. He watched her careful hands touch the knives and saucers; he thought her fingers were made of sun's rays.

They had a son, a boy of seventeen, and it was pleasant to have him about. Keith never wanted children. Children wasted one's time and grabbed one's money. Children were often sick or performed badly at school. Keith thought long about it. He should dedicate all his time to his brilliant collections. He could not leave them to a *museum*.

"It's much better for your personal effects to go to a son," Hilda said once.

He thought about it. Hilda would take care of the child. She'd bring it to doctors and she'd see to his problems at school. It turned out it was pleasant to have Patrick about. Keith saw him thirty minutes every day when the boy was clean and well fed. The child was not fussy. It sat in his chair while Keith read or cleaned his elephants. Patrick was well behaved and said, "Thank you" and "please." His clothes were clean and he never touched the objects of the collections with which Keith had forbidden him to trifle.

Keith travelled a lot. Sometimes Hilda accompanied him. Then the hotel room would be magnificent with the little odds and ends she dug out of nowhere, not many, two or three, no more; sometimes a seashell, a scarf, or an ancient book. Once, he had sent bouquets of flowers to women he had met on earlier occasions, so when he asked her to take a stroll around the neighborhood, she had looked at him directly in the eyes and refused. He needed and enjoyed that look; her pupils were whips of hate. It was such a pity that soon after that incident, she had gathered her things and returned to Brussels. She said that it was a matter of some urgency, which she would explain later, but she had to return.

"Do you need money?" Keith had asked once while dining at a posh restaurant. She replied in the negative, which had amused him. She never attempted to extract money or anything of value from him. If she'd tried, he'd have expelled her from his life. Hilda read his books. She liked the dishes he liked. She wore inexpensive clothes. And she was clean. At times, Keith thought that there were no traces of her presence around him. His shadow was her home and she lived there, unobtrusively like an autumn day. The look on his face told her what he wanted.

She was there for him, she did what was expected of her, and she satisfied his whims without seeming to mind. He liked to watch her touch his things. He loved it when she read his books. He asked her to write a few sentences about what had impressed her and she did. Her mind produced poisonous criticism, which attracted him because it contrasted bitterly her quiet words.

"You bad woman," he told her after he started collecting her acid remarks about the books he had bought. He enjoyed immensely her ability to see absurdity where there were no traces of it.

"I hate writing the catilinaires that you make me write," she said.

"Tell me what a catilinaire means," he said. He enjoyed her queer words, although he never told her he did. It was pleasant to bask in the scathing brilliance of her mind. He particularly liked it that it was his own exclusive pleasure. He didn't like the idea of somebody else enjoying the sting of her observations, the touch of her hands, the way she cooked the food. She was part of his collection and he hated the idea of others savouring his property.

"A spiteful piece of prose directed against somebody, that's what a catilinaire is," she said. "It's a French word."

"I know," he said. "Have you prepared Patrick's clothes for the camp in the Ardenes?"

"No," Hilda said.

He looked at her. "I think you don't care enough about your son," Keith said. "And I don't like that."

She didn't object to his accusation. She brought him a cup of orange juice. She always brought him orange juice when he'd done something she disliked.

"So it's true you don't care about Patrick?" he said. She didn't answer. He was suddenly angry but there was her silence. Her silences were the space where his anger died and peace began. Her jealousy was a foreign town he loved to explore, her discontent quiet skin betraying no anticipation. The depths of equanimity in her eyes exasperated him; the cup of orange juice on the table told him the truth. There were days when he felt victorious. He had broken down her defenses; he saw through her anger, although her face was a closed door.

"What is it this time?" he'd ask her.

"Nothing," Hilda would answer.

He tried to catch her out at the moment when she brought orange juice. It was a sign she was in a huff, but of course she throttled and erased all traces of her anger in a flash. Once, just once, he saw her open a bottle of orange juice and pour it into the kitchen sink.

This happened on the day when Keith took home Janette, the young translator who had worked on Keith's project to acquire a new hotel on the Northern Sea. Janette was all auburn hair and blue eyes, just about the average girl Keith chose for his collection he nicknamed 'Afternoons'. Hilda behaved immaculately as always. She talked politely to the translator about the mild winters in Brabant and the pleasant wind in the short summers. Keith noticed she drank orange juice all through the evening. He'd caught her unawares, her composure dead, the juice a pool of hate in her immaculately clean glass.

"You don't seem to like Janette," he said.

"I like her," Hilda answered pouring more orange juice into her glass.

"Did Janette tell you something?" Keith asked. He was not curious, he knew.

"She did," Hilda answered.

"She told you I was going to divorce you and marry her?"

"Yes," Hilda said.

Suddenly he hated her cold blood. He'd rather she screamed. He'd enjoy her fury. It was a dark devious street he'd love to explore. Her jealousy was the most precious piece of her.

"I wouldn't be so calm if I were you," Keith told her.

There was silence everywhere, cold and thick that Keith loved. He had to teach her a lesson. She had to respect him after all these years. She had to be at least a little jealous of him. Life was a sting of little jealousies that made days worth remembering. Hilda had to give him the spectacle of her life with him. He held this life like an intricate object that he could admire from many different angles. Possessed without complaint and silently enjoyed in studied contemplation. After all, she was obliged to respect him, wasn't she? He'd given her a home. He'd given her a roof and a child of whom she had to be proud.

"Janette is very clean," Hilda told him. "I don't worry about you."

"I'm glad you mentioned it," Keith said.

He adored order. Sloppiness and lack of method revolted him. Each woman he'd spent time with gave him a little present, though not one bought from a shop; he appreciated objects that were a part of his mistress's life. The objects that interested him were glimpses through a window into an afternoon where the woman enjoyed a cup of tea. He wanted that cup. There was a special hall in Keith's house in which he kept these selected afternoons. There were handkerchiefs, combs, postcards, silver buttons, and there were pieces of old newspaper smeared with lipstick. Hilda had attached little standard tags on each item. Jane, July 2007; Martha, August – November 2004; Gabriella, November 2000. Trying to tease him, she had added an umbrella with a tag that read, "John McLeod, July 2007. Keith was angry. In the beginning of August, he fired his associate John McLeod.

John McLeod was Janette's husband; Janette the translator.

Keith chose Janette carefully. He had to show Hilda he was not to be trifled with. He hated that umbrella and its silver tag with John's name, like a sprawling spider, on it. All the letters on that tag were insects that wove Hilda's cobweb about him. Her eyes were cobwebs, too. They held him. But, strangely enough, he would disrupt his internal composure by thoughts of her absence; how he would miss her when she was no longer part of his life, when he no longer possessed her life.

"Janette is different," Keith said to Hilda. "I won't have anything from her. She'll come to my house, and you'll have to go, I'm afraid."

Hilda kept her summer afternoons away from him. She remained a cold winter day and if she suddenly died she'd simply close the earth after her. That was all there was to it.

"I add an object to my 'Afternoons' collection after the girl leaves my life for good," Keith told her.

"I know that, "Hilda said.

"So, what will you give me?" he asked his eyes on her face.

She stood up walked to the refrigerator and took a bottle of orange juice.

Keith smiled. He liked it when Hilda drank orange juice. Then she gave him that prick of jealousy for which he had sought for so long.

"Yes, it's time I added something from you," he said.

Hilda didn't answer. The tired skin of her face remained unimpressed. This was a good sign. She drank the orange juice directly from the bottle. Keith felt strong, uproariously happy, and powerful, a man able to take and break.

The mahogany table glittered as Hilda placed the empty bottle on it.

"You can take that bottle," she said. "I'll write the necessary inscription on the tag for you."

"Well, Hilda," Keith said. "You know I'll never find another human being capable of taking care of my collections the way you do."

"That is a problem, isn't it?" she remarked, distant like the rainy night sky.

He suddenly hated the mahogany table, the thick carpet on the floor and the Brussels' autumn that appeared to be as slow to smile at him as her bland face.

"After we divorce I can hire you to look after my collections," Keith said. "You know every single object. You, like me, put your soul into collecting things."

She blushed, or was it his imagination? Was it the play of the lamp on the polished wood that made her face look taut?

"Another orange juice?" he asked.

Keith enjoyed every tiny breath of air suffused with the aroma of her uneasiness.

"Yes, please," Hilda said.

"I love the objects of my collections all the more because you've touched them," he said and he was telling the truth. "And I love it when you give me your chilly remarks on the books you've read."

Her smile was the crack through which he crept into the nights when she wanted him or when she hated him, which was one and the same thing with her.

"You can hire me to take care of your collections," Hilda said.

"Maybe I will," he said. "I'll let you know about my decision after I come back from Antwerp. The arts and crafts auction there, you know."

"I know," she said.

She might have asked him if Janette would accompany him to Antwerp. That would have given him a pleasant sensation. Hilda's rancor was a lake in which he'd love to have a swim. Hilda didn't ask him anything. She made it clear there would be no swim.

"I love the spiteful remarks you write about the books you've read. I laugh my head off as I read them."

"I wouldn't laugh if I were you," she looked at him, composed. "Give my love to Janette when you see her."

***

Keith came back home from the auction in Antwerp feeling exhilarated. He'd bought a china vase he intended to give Hilda. He knew she'd adore it. She'd been dreaming about a vase like that for years. Some objects of Keith's collections were her favorites, a Spanish sword from Seville she'd named Heart and a silver Portuguese clock she consulted every night. Keith gave that clock to Janette, and on the following day Hilda drank a gallon of orange juice. Then he gave Heart, the sword, to Janette. Hilda left the house saying she needed some time off. She said she'd stay at her favorite villa in Ostende, on the Northern

Sea, for a week, but Keith knew she didn't go anywhere. He'd followed her and he knew she stayed at the Metropole hotel, an ancient building from the Baroque period, famous for its drawings of swords that hung on the walls in the lobby.

***

He missed Hilda. Janette wanted to sell Heart, the sword, and the Portuguese clock to a museum. They belong there, Janette had said. She was young and ravishing. But she wanted to sell Heart! The idiot!

Keith imagined Hilda's astonishment the moment she'd see the sword in its usual place in the collection. That would be the perfect present for her birthday. Keith had missed her. And he looked forward to the aroma of his collections, to the glitter of his silver, the mystery of his malachite, to the sharpness of his weapons that Hilda had, no doubt, rearranged. She had her little surprises for him: she sneaked to admire Keith's favorite gold coins. She had dug out the history enveloping them; when Keith was depressed she read to him the stories about the Dutch nobleman who met his death as he tried to hide his gold from his cousins. These dark tales of disaster and woe calmed Keith down.

Keith kept Janette's electric toothbrush that was very good for her gums, the one with the gilded handle. That was an object Janette the translator loved, and it would be a part of the Afternoons collection. Janette was a toothbrush with a gilded handle; there were no dark tales of dead noblemen behind her. There was the bitter shame of her plan to sell Heart, the sword, and the Portuguese clock to a museum!

His house looked imposing against the azure of the sky. He loved his sitting room and his bedroom. He loved every inch of his manor. Hilda used to read to him disturbing tales of ancient Dutch nobleman. She'd cook for him and he'd watch the smooth, precise movements of her hands. He adored the evenings. Her body glided with the measured, noiseless movements of nameless women who had cooked centuries before her. She was a collector like him. She collected movements. He had planned to give her the Portuguese clock at midnight. Sex with her was fabulous after she saw the silver face and black fluorescent hands of the thing. Keith loved the sense of itching anticipation in his fingers every time Hilda's footsteps approached his bed.

He left the car in the garage and almost ran to the house. He opened the front door and was about to cry out "I'm home," when he noticed a big bottle of orange juice in front of the great mirror on the wall.

This was strange.

The antechamber was naked. The hat and coat rack had vanished, and the miniature marble sculptures of Venus and Apollo were gone. There was no carpet on the floor, and the small, carved redwood table that used to be in the corner under the frosted glass window had vanished. Keith ran to the living room and froze in his tracks. There were no tables and chairs, no TV set, no pictures on the walls, no shelves, and no books. The laptops were gone; the flowerpots were gone, while the divans and sofas had disappeared. The chandelier, which used to hang from the marble ceiling, was not there anymore. There was no trace of Keith's clay pipes he had arranged on the mantelpiece. The clock on the wall had vanished. The telephone was absent. There were no vases and no flowers in the room. There were no Spanish couches. Sheets of papers of different sizes and neatly arranged in equally big piles were stacked on the naked cement floor.

Keith stared stunned, unbelieving, his mouth gaping. There was a bottle of orange juice jutting out like a bad tooth in the middle of the circumference that the stacks of the documents formed.

He reeled, bent down, and amazed, shocked, tried to focus on one of the sheets of paper. It was a receipt, which read: Table, mahogany wood, 23 000 Euro. Then Keith read another piece of paper, Chair, mahogany wood, 17 300 Euro, then yet another one. They all were receipts. TV set, carpet, laptop, bookcase, a clay pipe, a silver sabre ....

He ran to the big rectangular hall where he kept his collections. But there were no collections. There were neat piles of papers with the word 'Euro' typed in red indelible ink. And there was a bottle of orange juice on the windowsill.

Keith groaned. He needed a drink. His brain squirmed and writhed. His heart exploded. The Afternoons collection with the presents he had received from the girls was there: a bottle of make-up and a brilliant silver tag on which Hilda had written in her round hand, Mary Jane,

February-March 2006; a cheap digital camera and a tag, arah, November 2007; a hairpin and "Judith, September 2008. There was an electric toothbrush with a gilded handle in Keith's coat pocket.

He needed a drink.

There was no refrigerator in the kitchen, no stove, no chairs, no table, and no booze.

There was a big crystal glass of orange juice on the marble floor.

MY HUSBAND THE SHOEMAKER

At the time about which I am going to tell you, Borko had not yet become the head of the veterinarian clinic in the town of Radomir. I saw him many times going for leisurely strolls—a twenty-three year old strapping fellow with a thin moustache and black smiling eyes.

I had a daughter, Radka. I gave birth to three sons before her—one after the other like beads of a rosary. They grew up sturdy guys, but when Radka came to life, my husband's eyes brimmed with tears of joy; he had his heart so much on having a daughter. Every time I gave birth to a son he gave me a kiss instead of a thank you.

My husband, who was my lord and my best friend, was a shoemaker. Day in day out, he cobbled old shoes and sandals for our neighbors and I took care of the children, the cows, the hens, and calves. Thank God, we had always had enough bread for everybody in the kitchen cupboard. It turned out the years I had waited for Radka were worth my while. She grew up very pretty, her eyebrows were thin like a tendril of a vine, and her eyes were warm. Our house was not a rich place, just a roof above our heads, but Radka shone like the proud sun.

Borko, the young vet, crossed our street seven or eight times a day, but he neither courted Radka nor spoke to her. So, I was calm. She was too young. The richest man in Radomir, whose estate touched the Greek border to the South, was called Kosta. He had a daughter, too. Her name was Adela. I wouldn't say Adela was a bad thing to look at; she was tallish, and pretty. Borko was said to be looking for a bride, so it was very easy to calculate that he'd choose Kosta's daughter.

No one doubted the match would be a success. Borko could cure sick cattle and made good money. Kosta, the big shot in town, wouldn't say no if the young vet volunteered to become his son-in-law. On the contrary, the old grouch would let every man drink a free bottle of brandy in his restaurant if that happened.

It was in the beginning of June that Kosta started hinting, "My stallion Thunderbolt is simply no good any more. I don't know what the matter with him is. He refuses to gallop when I ride him. The only living thing I love more than Thunderbolt is my daughter Adela."

So far so good. But the big land owner said something else that made young and old click their tongues. My neighbor, the baker's wife, told me that Kosta had stressed that, "If that greenhorn Borko cures my Thunderbolt, I'll let him marry Adela and I'll be as good as my word!"

The baker's wife told me that Borko went to Kosta's stables, examined the stallion carefully, slapped his back, nodded his head and said, "Mr. Kosta, your Thunderbolt is safe and sound. He is in exuberant health. Why did you call me out?"

"He's not safe and sound at all," the big bug seethed. "Don't you see the way his head's hanging low as if the blacksmith has clobbered him on the skull with the heaviest hammer?"

"You know better than me what your servants have done to your horse." Borko asked.

"What?" Kosta exploded.

"Your farmhands have been plucking wild poppies for a week now, Mr. Kosta. They must've made a concoction of poppies and rum and forced Thunderbolt to drink it. That's why the poor horse reels and staggers, and I'm positive that the blacksmith hasn't clobbered him on the head with the heaviest hammer."

"Who put that nonsense into your head?" Kosta shouted.

"One of your servants bragged to me the other day that you paid him ten levs for a basket full of wild poppies."

The landowner gaped; his eye looked bloodshot as if somebody had attached leeches on his neck. Finally he said, "Therefore you don't like Adela, eh?"

"I came here to cure your horse, Mr. Kosta," Borko answered. "Your daughter is blessed with beauty, I grant you that, but I cannot cure a healthy horse, Sir."

From that day on, whenever Kosta heard someone utter Borko's name in public, he took to mumbling under his breath, his face black like a bull's horn. The young vet couldn't care less. He went on taking long walks along our street. When occasionally I met him, I treated him to a piece of Turkish delight, and he didn't even glance at my daughter Radka. So I was calm.

"She's too young," my husband would always grumble, making me wonder how we'd separate from Radka one day when she'd get married.

36

Borko often came to my backyard to have a look at the calves, and we chatted away like old friends. I was a middle-aged woman and my neighbors said I had the gift of the gab.

The harvest began. We collected and drove home a big truck full of wheat. Life went on like a heavily loaded caravan, a happy day now and then, followed by many hungry weeks.

One day I noticed my daughter stole out of the house into the corn field, all alone. "Oh, come off it, girl!" I said to myself. "What will you be looking for in the wilderness?" But I was lazy to dig deep into that matter. On the following day, however, Radka again slipped out of our backyard into the same cornfield.

I shadowed her and lo and behold! I saw her pluck wild poppies. I said to myself, "Let's see what she'll do next." I was a shrewd woman. How could I hold a shoemaker of a husband in my house for twenty-four years while all other ladies in town, most of them younger and prettier than me, visited his shop and he measured how long and wide their feet were to make new shoes for them?

It was May 6th the following day, the holiday of courage. My three sons went out and my husband said he'd drop in the pub for a drink, only Radka, my daughter, hung about the sink in the kitchen very diligently washing the dishes. "Hey, mom, won't you visit your friend, the baker's wife? She said she baked cookies for you."

"I sure will," I answered, but instead of going out I slipped into the wine cellar. "Let me see what's eating her," I thought. Why should she be so keen on staying at home all alone on the very Day of Courage? Soon it was no mystery to me anymore. The little minx took out the wild poppies from the cupboard; put them into the biggest cauldron we had at home, poured all my husband's rum into it then kindled a big fire. The wild poppies boiled, hissed, and bubbled while I sweated in the cellar. Anyway, I managed to keep my mouth shut all the while.

After an hour, my pretty daughter mixed the foul smelling concoction with water, then brought Marko, our loyal donkey, and made the poor creature drink the nasty thing. Marko didn't want to dip its mouth in the poison; he kicked and jumped, and spat, but I knew something for sure, the poor animal could not outdo my Radka in mulishness? No, not by a long shot!

She pressed Marko's head, scratched his back and gave him half a bag of sugar till she wheedled the wretched beast into slurping the smelly slops. In the very beginning, Marko tried to turn a somersault, then he threw his head back and started braying most powerfully. After a couple of minutes, however, the beast prostrated himself in the middle of the backyard, kicked feebly twice and became quiet. I was afraid our only donkey was about to meet his maker very soon. Radka, the child I loved more than everything in the world, abandoned the sick animal and went out accompanied by three or four other girls as flighty as she was, while the donkey was on his deathbed!

My husband, my lord and best friend, came home from the pub. He was tipsy and merry, but when the sight of the dying Marko met his eye, his hands flew to his heart in despair. What could we do? We had no other choice and called Borko, the vet.

There he came and entered my backyard, a real hunk, his eyes agleam, and my Radka dilly-dallied by the hen-coop feeding the hens. In fact, the vet didn't even notice her, if you asked me. He bent over the donkey, slapped his back, and pulled on his tail. Finally he said, "It is very serious, Sir. Your beast of burden will die."

"How come he dies?" I asked for I knew very well what was wrong with Marko. "Yesterday the animal was as strong as the cliffs on the hill behind our house."

"Well, yes, he might have been perfectly healthy an hour ago, but there is a very dangerous disease the donkey in our area suffer from, you know," Borko said. "I will try to cure him, but ..." He left the words hanging in grim silence.

"Why do you say "but"?" my husband asked.

Borko didn't answer him.

My friends knew I liked to take occasional naps in the afternoon; I was a mother of four so I hoped nobody would call me a lazy woman. One day I was just about to doze off when I caught a glimpse of something that struck me as very peculiar: Borko, the vet, gave my youngest son a bulging sack and the boy took an armful of wild poppies out of it. The following day our wretched Marko could neither eat nor bray any more. We gave up all hope so we sent for Borko.

The young vet came and said to my husband, "Well, Sir, I'll make Marko alive and kicking, but perhaps you remember what Mr. Kosta offered to give me if I cured his Thunderbolt."

"I do," my husband answered. "He offered you Adela."

"You have a daughter as well," Borko ventured.

My husband shouted, "Give me a knife to cut this crook's throat!" and after that cussed a lot, using lousy words.

After two weeks, our donkey recovered his health. It was at that time that Radka got engaged to Borko, although she was too young. On that day, my husband, my lord and my best friend, was stricken with grief and drank himself stone drunk. I thought it was the happiest day in my life and drank myself drunk with joy by his side.

LENTIL SOUP

Her apartment was small and she heated only one room in it. She said she had to be very economical; she had to save up money. All men are like you, she said. You come and go when you please and can I rely on you? Not really.

It always rained when he walked along the street where she lived. It was narrow and dank. The facades of the houses were gray slabs of mold and old age. There were no trees in the neighborhood, but the rents were low and she was happy, she said. She added she loved the street when it rained. That particular night, she put on her old coat and went out, and he remained in the room staring at the sky. Later she told him the night and the sky were twins and she couldn't tell one from the other.

"Angelika, you are out of your mind" he had said, but she just smiled at him or maybe at the mist.

What was she happy about Dietrich wondered. What on earth made her so happy in the cold city where no one cared for her? She came back home wet, frozen and grinned at him. He didn't ask where she'd been. Her face was pale and wan, but she said she loved him and she loved the warm room in her apartment.

I can fix you something to eat, she said, and took to cooking a lentil soup in which she put wild mint and vinegar. He waited for her meal watching her arms sparkle amidst the enormous delicious smell of her casserole.

"I love it when you are here," Angelika said. "I'm lazy and I wouldn't cook for myself. But things change when you say you are hungry."

He ate a bowl of soup, and she told him it was good to have him about. "Look at the rain. It is coins filling your purse," she added. "Let's go and pick them."

They went out in the street and kissed under the silver coins of her rain, the smallest room in her apartment waiting for them. "That's a poky place," she said. "But it changes when you are here. It feels like summer, doesn't it?"

When on the following day the sun in the sky was a yellow rusty patch among the clouds, she said, "It's an old song, that's what that sun is. Look at the street. Today the houses glow. So let's go and have a beer at the "Kleiner Weinkeller". It's open now."

The Kleiner Weinkeller, or the Small Wine Cellar, was the cheapest pub in Gladbach. The beer in it was a magic and cost only one Euro a pint, she explained.

"Listen, I can call in sick," she said. "Just think about it. You come to see me so rarely. I should be crazy if I let you stay all alone in that drizzly Gladbach all day long."

She worked in a translation office in Alter Stadt, the Old Town, and she said she loved it—her office was so spacious and warm compared to her flat. She was constantly broke. She squandered the money she made on long cheap excursions to different cities in Belgium: Liege and Namur, and Charleroi, and dozens of unknown small towns.

"You should see their cathedrals," she said. "You'll be crazy about the luminous space above them. And there's splendid beer. The guys in the old breweries know different tricks. I enjoy the fog in the abbeys. Believe it or not, that fog is two thousand years old. Here, take little sip of this one. This beer is unique. I brought a bottle for you from the abbey of Wurzellen."

The beer was weak and he said it was no good.

"Why don't you ask me where I go when I'm not with you? All women want to know that," he teased her. "I tell them about you, Angelika. They are mad when I praise your lamb casserole and your lentil soup."

"I can understand that," she said nodding her head. "My lamb casserole is great. Well, the important thing is I'm not broke right now. You brought in so much money. We can go to Lava restaurant and eat a dinner there."

"No Lava restaurant," he said. "You fix me something to eat here. I love it here."

She didn't grumble and her kitchen was soon a jungle of beautiful smells, roasted lamb, buttered potatoes, orange juice and white yeast bread she fried in a big pan on the plate. He didn't want to go to the small abbeys with their famous beer. He had seen Waterloo and the Citadel in Namur. He didn't care about the famous room with the tilting floor in the Citadel which made you feel dizzy. He wanted the sweet smell of her narrow room. Then he wanted his job and his car. He built roads and houses, he was somebody out there and he thought Belgium and northern France were quiet places which didn't attract him. He had worked everywhere—in Madrid and in Marseilles, in Dublin and in Oostende. He had built the TV center in Amsterdam and he had designed the Hayat Tower of Light in Istanbul. He built the *gaudron*, the endless asphalt road in Mauritania. He built one of the suspension bridges over the Maas River in the Netherlands.

"Really?" she didn't believe him when he said he liked the orange curtains at her place. "This is the neighborhood with the lowest rents in Monchengladbach. I know you come back here not because of the curtains but because of me."

"Not because of you," he told her. He'd always been honest to women and he hated it when they started planning and building a future for him.

"Oh, of course it's me you come here for," she said smiling. "You just don't know it yet." He liked her smile. "In Monchengladbach, I make the big difference, Dietrich."

"I love the smells of your kitchen," he said. "And I like the way you spend my money. You are very economical."

"O, shut up," she said. "You should say I'm pretty and you can't live without me. Tell me you can't smoke without me. My heart will melt like a candy if you say that."

"But you are not pretty and I can smoke quite well without you," he said. "And besides, what will you do if your heart melted?"

"Come to think about it I'd rather take you to the warm room."

"I'd rather you made an apple strudel for me," he said.

"Aha," she said. "I know what you are up to. When you start speaking of apple strudels the next thing you do is pack up all your things. Then you are gone. Let's go to the warm room."

He didn't object. He liked her skin. It smelled sweet like her kitchen. He liked the way she went to sleep easy, and he liked her question "When will you come back? If I know the day in advance, I'll make a broccoli quiche for you."

"I'll tell you what you'll make for me when I come," he said.

What she didn't know was that his favorite vacations were the time he spent with her. When his friends asked him, "Where did you go, Dietrich?" he'd answer, "I stayed with my mother for a week." His mother cooked like her.

"If you have an important letter to send me, which says you miss me, send it to my mother," he told Angelika and gave her the old lady's address. "Don't write too often ,though. My mother collects my correspondence for me and grumbles if she has to walk to the post box twice a day."

He half expected she'd get angry. She smiled at him and said, "Okay. Thanks for giving me that precious address."

"And what was the weather like in Rome?" one of his colleagues wanted to know after Dietrich came back to work. Dietrich had not visited Rome. He was in her warm room, with the miracle of her lentil soups.

"It rained all the time," he answered, thinking of the gray streets. But the silver coins of the rain were still in his purse. He remembered the asphalt squares of the ancient German town. They are the color of the eyes of a man in love, Angelika had said.

"I love the town," she said. "It's so clean, and I like the sun. I even like the Hauptbahnhoff—the old railway station, you know. Its noise is beautiful when you are here."

"It's because I leave you a lot of money," he pointed out.

"Yes," she agreed. "I'm not broke. In fact, I am the richest woman in the neighborhood. Where have you been all this time? In Lisbon or in Athens?" But she didn't wait for him to answer. "You look good. You do. You feel like broccoli quiche?"

They walked in the rain. Her street was mercury she said, and he'd better keep his eyes open. One didn't see such a street every day.

As always, he went away without warning.

"Women in Gladbach are easy going," she wrote in a letter Dietrich's mother received. "There's endless spring washing away my blues. You know, I was sick a week ago. I thought I'd die. I wished you were here. Thank Cod it was nothing serious. Next time I'll fix you a pumpkin pie. They make nice pumpkin pies in Bonn, and I got the recipe from an old lady. I look forward to baking it for you."

The next time when he came to Monchengladbach it was raining again. There was so much mercury in the streets that the gray houses were ready to run to the Abbey of Wurzellen. The oldest brewery in Nord Rhein Westfalen Province, and hopefully in Germany, was there.

He looked forward to her quiche, and to the orange curtains on the windows. He looked forward to her skin that had the Gladbach rains in it.

He rang the bell at the front door and waited. No one showed up, but he was not worried. Often, she was not at home on Sundays. She rode her bike to Wickrath where the shops for used cars were. She'd been constantly on the lookout for a cheap old Volkswagen Polo. He had half a mind to buy her one so she'd stop babbling about buying and selling used cars.

She was sure to come back home soon. Dietrich went to have a drink in the Kleiner Weinkeller where the barman nodded to him. No one opened the door when he tried the bell after a couple of drinks more. He loved the quiet pub she'd taken him so often. Dietrich noticed she had not drawn the orange curtains. He wondered who he could ask after her. He didn't know anybody in Monchengladbach but her silver rain.

After a week he visited his mother. A letter waited for him. He recognized the careful oval outlines of the words. She had tried to teach him French spelling in the Kleiner Weinkeller and he said her handwriting was a string of clouds.

Her letter said,

Dearest Dietrich,

I will not live in Monchengladbach any more. I'll marry Adelbert Kess. I translated one of his novellas and he said he liked my translation. I don't enjoy making apple strudels for him. I loved every minute of your time with me. There will be no silver in the rains without you. I was afraid of living alone, you know. I often think we didn't have time for your broccoli quiche.

Loving you,
Angelika.

THE OLD HOUSE

Ena's grandfather Goran built the house sixty years ago. He was a powerful merchant and traded in wheat, medicines, cotton and wool, which he exported to Romania. He had made heaps of money even before the cholera epidemics struck. In the troubled times during the World War II, he took to his heels, hid in Romania and fell in love with a Romanian woman there. He dumped Ena's grandmother, Mladena, and the woman pined away slowly, alone in the unfinished house. He had built the roof above the rooms, true, but there were no doors or windows, and the brick walls had had not been plastered. Goran and Mladena had no children. That was the main reason why he took all the money and beat it to Austria, or perhaps to Italy with that Romanian beauty. He badly wanted an heir, he had often said. The Romanian woman, in Mladena's opinion, was by no means pretty, just a prattling Gypsy who made eyes at her husband.

Grandma Mladena found herself broke. She came into possession of two wardrobes of fine Austrian suits, two suitcases stuffed with dresses, and a house with a dozen spacious rooms with high ceilings which, in winter, froze with cold that no stove in the world could drive away. The neglected wife hung her head in shame. She became the talk of the town and, having no official documents, she couldn't sell the enormous building; actually, not a building but several dozen gaping walls.

Mladena tried to sell her dresses. Nobody wanted a barren woman's clothes—your daughter wouldn't conceive and the whole town would jabber about that. Then Mladena started selling her husband's suits. She attracted a few customers; Goran was a big shot in these parts, and his name was as good as gold in your purse. Mladena hoped that a bricklayer or a plasterer would buy her husband's Austrian jackets. She put a sheet of paper on the front door: **I sell half-price suits to plasterers**. But you would find no plasterers in that town, where people made their houses of wattle and daub. Finally a man came to see the Austrian garments.

"I am a plasterer," he said. "Give me one of these half-price suits."

"If you really are a plasterer I'd like you to put plaster the walls and ceilings of my house," she said. "I'll let you live in the cellar or in that small room over there. But you'll have to plaster the kitchen first. I'll cook for you. You appear to be poor. I will sell Goran's household goods and I'll pay you."

That plasterer gave Mladena the once-over and said, "Your neighbors told me your husband dumped you because you couldn't have a child. Listen, I'm looking for a woman exactly like you. I won't squander money on tarts while I plaster your house. Do I make myself clear? We'll live together, you'll cook for me and you'll wash my clothes. I'll plaster the walls and I'll put in windows, too. If you agree, let's do it. If I like you, I'll start plastering right away."

Mladena said, "But there's not even a bed here."

"So? The floor will do. Don't waste my time. If I don't like you, I'll leave five leva. I never leave a woman more than a fiver. If I like you, I'll plaster the kitchen."

He left her a fiver and made himself scarce, but after a week he came again and took to plastering. The man gave up after a couple of days, left another fiver on the kitchen floor and decamped from the house, dressed in one of Goran's suits, a pair of Goran's sandals on his feet. After a month he came back, but Goran's suit and Goran's sandals were gone. The man wore shorts, even though this June was cold. He'd lost his garments gambling, he said. Then Rafko, that was his name, got down to plastering again, but he often needed Mladena's help. He told her she'd better spread a blanket on the floor "every now and then", and he'd leave a fiver for her. The problem was he had no money, but she could calculate how much he owed her. Rafko ate up all the bread and cheese in the house, and there were no potatoes or turnips in the cellar. Mladena didn't have a penny to bless herself with. She had already sold Goran's suits, Goran's shoes, Goran's chairs and Goran's cupboards, so she really counted on the thirty-seven fivers the plasterer owed her. The only thing she hadn't sold was a sewing machine; she planned to pawn it. If worse came to worst, she intended to pull down the house and sell the bricks. She hoped to live off the bricks until she found a widower with little children. The woman reckoned she could take care of the kids and eke out a living with their father.

One day, Mladena grew desperate and put another advertisement on a piece of cardboard, **I sell half-price SINGER sewing machine to a widower with little children.**

Meanwhile Rafko plodded along, plastering the living room, but his trowel left humpbacked or cracked walls in its wake. When there was no more food in the kitchen, he stole potatoes and onions from other gardens, or he gambled. Mladena couldn't tell for sure. Sometimes in the evening, he brought loads of food in black plastic sacks: muddy potatoes lay on top of loaves of bread, occasional chocolates, or sausages; you could find all that in Rafko's roomy bags. He gorged himself on peppers, olives, and cookies thrust into his mouth all at once. The more he ate the less he plastered, spending most of his time with Mladena on her only blanket. One day he suggested, "Listen, I'd better stop paying you. I've already fallen into your ways. You are as meek as a ewe. I'll plaster your house for free and instead of living in the cellar I'll move in with you. I'll treat Priest Mano to a glass of brandy; he'd marry us for fee. We won't go to the church. He'll marry us in front of the SINGER, do you agree? Then I can go when I am fed up with you, and God won't be cross with me."

He lied to Mladena. He didn't treat Priest Mano to a glass of brandy; he borrowed twenty leva from him instead. Rafko said he wanted to buy a wedding ring for his bride. He lied again, of course. He bought a tuxedo, a tie and a bed. A German engineer fell ill and soon met his maker. The plasterer took the tux and the tie from the man's body for three leva—dirt cheap indeed—then stowed away the bed the engineer had died in. Rafko promised the German widow to dig a grave for her husband in return for the bed. Of course, no one ever saw that grave.

Actually, Priest Mano couldn't finish the marriage ceremony. Halfway through it the plasterer said, "Stop. That's enough. I don't have money enough for more. Don't make a face at me, Priest Mano. It gets on my nerves! If you make a face again, I'll strip your cassock and sell it to buy Mladena a wedding ring. Do you get my meaning?"

The priest raised hell but Rafko the plasterer clutched him by the throat and started taking off the black cassock. At a certain point, he said, "Actually, nobody would buy your smelly coat, anyway," so he kicked the priest's ass and rushed home to his wife, who had already spread the blanket on the dead German's bed.

Soon, there was no more bread in house again, but Rafko didn't mind.

"For the first time in my life I don't have to pay a woman," he sighed happily, smiling at the gray, still unplastered walls. Rafko sold the SINGER sewing machine and bought three bags of flour, onions and potatoes. He wanted Mladena all the time. After a week, the flour was gone, but he said potatoes would do.

"We have to repair the house," Mladena remembered.

"Take it easy, woman," he roared. "Some time or other I'll plaster the house, to hell with it! Mladena, you are here now, let's grasp this opportunity. Think about me! If you die, what shall I do? I have to search for another woman. Do you think I can find a meek one like you? Not even if I wore out ten pair of boots looking for her."

"Hey, Rafko," Mladena said one day. "May period is late. Maybe I'll have a baby."

"So what?" he said. "You are not dead yet, are you? Let's seize this opportunity! Don't even think of going out, woman. Well, I'd prefer it if you were barren. But you look pretty to me. If the baby is pretty and healthy, we can sell it for fifty leva to some childless couple."

When Mladena gave birth to a baby girl the townspeople exclaimed, "Wow! That Mladena wasn't barren at all!"

The Romanian beauty Goran had eloped with returned to Bulgaria, found Mladena and said, "Listen, Goran, may worms feast on his liver, kicked me out because I couldn't have a baby. But you have to know, Mladena, it's all his fault. His seed is no good. It's rotten. Look at you. You gave birth to a baby as big as a calf. I have no roof over my head, Mladena, I'm flat broke. Will you let live in your house with you? You and I will plaster the walls together."

The walls again remained unplastered. Rafko made the Romanian beauty sell first her dress, then her bracelet. After that she pawned her shoes and the two of them drank and sang a couple of weeks in the cellar. Finally, Rafko moved in with her "for good". Everything between them was okay while there was bread and cheese in Rafko's bags. The beauty started shouting dirty words in Romanian at him. Once she tied him to the bed, where he had fallen asleep, and thrashed him with his own belt, repeating, "Give me the 96 fivers you owe me!"

The next day, Rafko threw the beauty out into the street with only her nightgown on, poor soul. Then he went to his wife's room, took his baby girl in his hands and started to sing to it. That was one thing the plasterer was good at. God had blessed him with a beautiful voice. The roosters stopped crowing while he sang to the baby in the morning, and the rooks didn't caw in the poplar trees when he crooned a lullaby to her at night. Rafko soon tired of the baby, though, and took off again. After a month or so, he came back to Mladena.

"I can live only with you. You are an angel. An archangel even, and know it." He bowed down before her and kissed her knees. "The Romanian vixen tried to cut my throat twice. She gave me rat poison, too, and I puked up my dinner. She burned all my underwear. Nasty virago! But you are an angel! Yes, you are, Mladena!" he whispered and kissed her knees once more.

Then Rafko started plastering the walls again, but not with much success. His eyes were on Mladena all the time. He often got down from the scaffolding and said to her, "Hang around me just in case. We can take advantage of the opportunity, you know." From time to time he told her she was an angel, and in the evenings he sang to the baby. He held the little girl, smiled and said, "What a pretty child! She's Daddy's little beauty! "

Then Rafko took to singing and dancing at weddings and at birthday parties. At the end of the day, he brought bags of broiled chickens or pork chops, cheese and sometimes even a bundle of five-leva banknotes. Mladena couldn't tell for sure if he'd stolen it all. He bought the baby expensive clothes and never said another word about selling her to a childless couple.

Rafko again vanished into thin air and the neighbors hinted to Mladena that Rafko had eloped to Sofia with a young ballerina. The ceilings and walls of the house remained bare, but now there were windows and doors everywhere. Mladena regularly cleaned a wealthy man's stables and washed his wife's clothes. Although people in Pernik were as sensitive as paving stones, once in a blue moon they gave her old clothes for her baby girl. Actually, Mladena had already found her feet when Goran came back home. He looked wealthier than ever, arriving in a dazzling German car. Goran got out of it and saw Mladena's daughter crawling on the front lawn.

"I know what you did while I was away," Goran said to his wife. "It's okay. I'll take you back with the kid."

Perhaps he knew his seed was no good and he could beget nothing but fat bundles and bank accounts. He hired bricklayers, master masons and plasterers; he had the place surrounded with stone walls and nailed gold and silver Austrian rattles above the toddler's cot.

One day while Goran was at work, Rafko the plasterer came back to the town, and lo and behold he couldn't believe his eyes. Mladena's place was surrounded with a wall, her house was roofed with marble slabs, and the walls looked as if fresh snowflakes had fallen on them an hour ago! He made up his mind to go in and check out what had happened, but at the moment he touched the front door two mutts as big as donkeys descended on him, growling and snarling. "Their throats are deep as caves," Rafko thought, but caves or no caves he went for it. Mladena came out to see what the commotion was. He saw her, jumped eagerly, and shouted, "Let me kiss your knees! You are an angel! An archangel! I wore out twenty pairs of boots looking for a woman like you. Wow! There's no other like you! Take my word for it. Listen, I've got a bag of bread and cheese here. Find a blanket quickly. I can't wait, woman."

"My husband's coming home from work," Mladena said. "He whitewashed the house and put new doors and windows."

"What husband?" Rafko seethed. "Didn't Priest Mano marry us? And whose ass did I kick so he'd get lost and I could kiss you? Mladena, didn't you tell me 'With this ring I thee wed'?"

"But I didn't have a ring," Mladena said.

"So what? Who is the father of the kid in the yard, eh?"

"I tell you, Goran is here," Mladena said. "Go away or he'll shoot you dead."

"We'll see about that!" Rifko said.

Then he tossed some bones to the mutts, hugged the toddler to him and started to sing. A voice as beautiful as the sun poured out of his lips. Mladena forgot that he had sold her SINGER sewing machine, ignored the fact he had left her in the lurch with the baby. She forgot she'd had to clean cow dung all winter. She just listened to Rafko's song. The baby listened, too.

"Come on," Rafko told her. "You know what we're going to do."

"No way, "Mladena said. "We can't do that. Goran is coming home. Take the money and go," she said and gave him a roll of banknotes. After Goran returned, there was money stored in all drawers in the kitchen.

"Listen, come here and forget about the money. If by chance you die, then what! You are all right now, so let's take this opportunity."

They didn't stop taking this opportunity until night fell. Then Mladena fed her daughter and Rafko sang to her. He sang and sang as if he had the music of ten hearts in his chest. Goran worked long hours that day. When finally he came home, Rafko and Mladena were about to take the opportunity again, celebrating the fact Mladena was alive. Rafko was saying "There's no other like you!" when he was aware something had gone wrong. A gun was pressed to the back of his skull.

"What are you doing here?" Goran roared.

"Can't you see what I'm doing?" Rafko retorted. "Are you blind? Listen, either kill me with that gun or let me get back to my business!"

Goran flew into a rage and shot. Fortunately for Rafko, he had aimed at the ceiling.

"I sang to the child," Rafko shouted. "I made a family for you. Now you have a daughter to leave your money to, you idiot."

Goran shot once again. His bodyguards rushed into the room like hounds. The next day the neighbors found pools of Rafko's blood and wisps of his brown hair all along the street near Goran's house.

"Put on your clothes," Goran ordered Mladena that night. "If I catch you again with him ... See this?" He showed her the big kitchen knife. "I'll cut your throat with it. You know I slaughter cows and lambs, so be careful."

Mladena looked at the marble slabs on the floor.

"Will you throw me out?" she asked.

"Yes," he said.

He didn't throw her out, though. He hired a neighbor to feed and lull the baby to sleep and took Mladena to the cellar where he kept Rafko's tuxedo and tie, the ones that had belonged to the dead German engineer.

"Did that schmuck sing to you?" Goran asked his wife.

"Yes, he did," Mladena said.

"Then I'll sing to you, too," Goran declared. He opened his mouth and thundered out a couple of words. Mladena thought she heard five oxen moo, a bulldog snarl and fireworks splutter. The rooks flew away from the poplar trees, terrified; the roosters crowed even though it was past midnight, and the baby wailed bitterly.

"Does he sing better than me?" Goran asked.

"Yes, he does," Mladena answered.

"But he dumped you!" Goran shouted.

"You dumped me before he did, "Mladena said.

Goran took out a fat wad, laid the banknotes on her pillow and said, "He didn't have this! You cleaned cow dung and washed dirty underpants!"

"He kissed my knees," Mladena said.

"Well, I won't kiss your knees," Goran said and put on the tuxedo and the tie.

"Did he look better than me?" Goran asked his wife.

"Yes, he did," Mladena said.

The Romanian beauty came to beg money from Goran, but he set the dogs on her, then took the rifle from the wall to shoot at her. Fortunately for the Romanian, Mladena was there. She gave her bread and some ten-leva bills in an old purse.

"You are a good woman," the beauty said and kissed Mladena's cheeks. "Listen, Goran's bodyguards broke Rafko's legs. Now he's in Sofia and he's a beggar. Give me some more money. I'll find him and I'll help him."

Mladena gave her more ten-leva bills.

***

Mladena's daughter was very pretty from an early age. Crowds of boys thronged to see her and tell her she was the most beautiful girl they had ever seen. The stone wall that surrounded Goran's house was covered with flowers. Young men wrote on it, **I love you,** in their own blood. Goran looked at the girl, sighed happily and could not believe his eyes. Young men trampled the grass around his house and trod dozens of paths to her window. She was the queen of the town and every day chose another young man, usually the one who brought her the most expensive necklace.

At seventeen, Goran's pretty adopted daughter gave birth to a baby girl, Ena by name. She couldn't tell who the father was—he might have been anyone. Then Rafko's daughter left the baby with Grandma Mladena and Grandpa Goran and went to live in Sofia.

By that time, grandpa Goran was not a rich merchant anymore. He was an old man who suffered from rheumatism, and the bones in his body felt like a mouthful of bad teeth. Goran often played chess with another old man, Grandpa Rafko, lame in the left leg. In the evenings, the two geezers drank brandy together, and when the night was warm, the one with the lame leg sang in a beautiful voice. Mladena thought he still had the power and the music of ten hearts in his chest. Grandpa Goran, although his rheumatism tortured him, sang, too. In fact, he roared, and wailed, and sputtered as if he had an excavator in his throat, trying to dig a ditch in the street. Mladena thought Goran wanted to frighten her away from the room where the two of them got drunk. However, Grandma Mladena didn't scare easily. She sat opposite the two men, even though she was sleepy, her legs hurt and every square inch of them hurt, but she cooked for the men and poured brandy into their glasses. Sometimes she watched a silly TV show for a change.

Young Ena was a quiet child, beloved by all who knew her: Grandpa Rafko with his angelic voice, Grandpa Goran and Grandma Mladena. The three of them were always by Ena's side, and the baby never wailed or sobbed. She grew up a most tractable child—quieter than the roof tiles, more tranquil than the air in the cellar where no one lived. The four of them lived in the same old house that summers filled with youth and winters with the most beautiful silver one could dream of.

IT'S YOUR TURN

Eleanor Cunningham was an exceptionally cold-blooded woman. Her eyes narrowed as she stared at a small, crumpled newspaper clipping. Her fingers trembled with suppressed rage. She had found the clipping in her husband's wallet during one of her regular searches. It was an advertisement, carefully underlined by Henry. There could be no doubt that Henry himself had done that. He had used the platinum pen kept especially for signing company mergers and the most important contracts of the week. There was something else: that pen was his talisman.

Henry Cunningham was one of the richest men in North America, renowned for his fabulous wealth and the unbelievable sums of money he squandered gratifying his whims. Such a man, soberly noted Eleanor, would not waste time reading advertisements in gossipy newspapers. Yet the clipping was in her hands and Henry had saved it in his wallet.

Wild Life Ltd Works For Influential People.

As Eleanor read further, her face gradually lost its color.

We can transform every courageous person into any living being they fancy. Do you dream of becoming a lion?

Do you want to feel the power?

You can!

Are you yearning to experience the ferocity of a shark?

Your dream can come true with our help!

Would you like to discover why a dog is loyal to its master?

Here is the answer!

We guarantee impunity of your acts while you are a free wild being.

Wild Life Ltd challenges the brave: free yourself from your restricting human skin, find your selfhood, your true nature!

Wild Life Ltd is the only organization offering you a way out!

Eleanor Cunningham did not need to read the advertisement to the end. An unpleasant thought had crossed her mind. "Oh, Henry", she murmured, "you have really made up your mind this time."

The private detective, Eleanor Cunningham, originally hired had explained to her in unambiguous phrases that Sir Henry often visited 5

Dove Street—a magnificent snow—white house where the famous ballerina Florence Hughes lived. She was devastatingly beautiful and had been a valuable companion for him at receptions and parties for five successive seasons. On hearing the detective's report, Eleanor Cunningham had began to surreptitiously check her husband's personal papers and wallet.

It was the last Friday of May when Eleanor discovered the newspaper advertisement. She had a thought that sent a shiver along her spine: Is this why Henry has been on a severe diet for three weeks? Why is he having nothing but orange juice day and night? What is he up to?

Eleanor then visited Doctor Burrows who had taken care of her husband's health since Henry's birth. "Do not worry, Mrs. Cunningham", the doctor said with a non-committal smile. "Sir Henry is extremely healthy. His body is strong, well trained and needs only a minimal diet."

Henry Cunningham had ceased eating. He had decided to turn into another being; a tiger, a lion, a hyena. Another affordable whim. The turnover of his companies exceeded a quarter of a billion on a daily basis. So *Wild Life* was the latest quirk of Elinor's eccentric husband.

On the very same evening Eleanor Cunningham found the advertisement, she started taking lessons to shoot at a moving target. She had not breathed a word about it, not even to her closest friend Susan, Chair of the Duchess' Club. In the beginning Elinor practiced with a safari gun, before deciding on an exquisite revolver. Meanwhile, she tried to draw out her husband.

"Henry, don't you think that a single glass of orange juice is not enough for you to keep body and soul together? You are a big, strong man, darling."

Sir Henry's features contracted into a peculiar ferocious expression. Within a split second his white teeth flashed, radiating a sharp bloodthirsty glow.

"Do not worry about me, darling," he said, his eyes avoiding hers.

Elinor was not worried at all. She had slipped her dainty revolver under the silky pillow on her bed. The polished metal surface glinted gently in the gloom of the baroque bedroom. A second revolver lay expertly hidden in a vase just outside the parlor. Elinor was now prepared for any ferocious beast crouching in the shadows of her home.

Today is the day, Elinor thought. She dropped an empty glass on the tile floor and collected the shards herself. She did not want servants to witness what she was about to do. As Elinor bent to kiss Henry goodnight that evening, she let the sharp pieces of broken glass pierce his hand. His tanned skin shone with a coppery warmth as it began to bleed.

Strangely, for a moment, it seemed a droplet of water shimmered there also, apparently unwilling to mingle with Sir Henry's blood.

"I am so sorry, dear," Elinor whispered softly. Henry's face lit with that distant, peculiar smile, his sharp teeth gleaming.

"Forget it, my love", he muttered softly.

The full moon shone into the bedroom. Henry Cunningham's bed was empty. The sheets and the blankets were rolled in a mess, strewn with short, russet hairs.

Elinor woke in fright as the long, pointed claws of a bulldog tore at her nightclothes. Her shoulder was bleeding. The muzzle of the beast was smeared with her blood and its jowls gaped open hungering for her throat. The glowing teeth of that enormous head swung above her face and for a moment reminded Eleanor of someone very familiar.

"That's you, Henry!" she shouted and bucked and twisted, seizing the gun. A muffled shot. A low growling moan filled the air before the heavy bulldog slumped limp across Elinor's chest. The miniature revolver was hot and still smoking in her hand.

Nine days later, Henry Cunningham, the fabulously rich owner of petrol refineries, was slowly regaining his strength in a luxury hospital room. His body was weak yet the readings of the medical equipment were encouraging. Sir Henry, in Doctor Burrows's opinion, would soon recover. The doctor had tactfully retreated leaving three people in the room: Henry, beautiful Florence Hughes and Mr. Brinkley, a representative of *Wild Life Ltd.*

"Sir", ventured Brinkley timidly. "I hope you are satisfied with our service despite the little accident you had. The doctors say your wound is healing well." The official of *Wild Life Ltd* pursed his lips in a plaintive funnel searching for another excuse.

"I am satisfied," Henry Cunningham answered curtly. "This is for you." At the sight of the sum written on the cheque, a broad smile lit Brinkley's face. Ignoring it, Sir Henry said impatiently, "You can go now."

Nothing in the tycoon's voice betrayed the fact that he had survived a bullet. He was being taken care of by the best team of doctors in the country, and in ten days time would be up and about as promised. Yes, there was a powerful reason to be impatient: Florence Hughes. She sat on the edge of his bed, smiling wistfully, gently dabbing the beads of perspiration on Henry's forehead.

"Dear Florence," Henry whispered lovingly. "Your idea was brilliant. I ... I am done with Eleanor. She is no more. There will be no sleuths dogging us everywhere. The world will leave us alone at last."

"God bless Eleanor," the beauty whispered piously. "Perhaps she's already on her way to Heaven."

Henry Cunningham was happy. He had often asked himself how Flo was able to transform each word she pronounced into magic. That magnificent woman was worth everything.

As Henry summoned the nurse to bring some food, Florence remarked: "The police haven't discovered Eleanor's body yet. They found several bones and that was all."

"Perhaps the bulldog was not hungry enough and left them for later on", Henry noted calmly. For a moment his teeth shone with a sharp, weird luster. "Let's not talk about Eleanor anymore." He stroked the hand of his beautiful ballerina.

At that moment the door of the room opened and an elderly nurse stood in the dim rectangular patch of light.

"This is for you, Sir," she said, handing Sir Henry a small, expensive cassette recorder. "And, if it is possible, Sir, Mr Brinkley from *Wild Life* would like to discuss it with you afterwards."

Puzzled, Henry took the recorder.

"Leave the room!" he ordered the nurse. He switched on the machine; the wheels turned slowly. Then Henry gave a violent start as Eleanor's voice came through the microphone.

"Dear Henry, when I found the *Wild Life* advertisement, I understood instantly that you were up to no good. Of course, it was quite difficult for me to stomach the idea that you would turn yourself into some sort of beast to be rid of me."

Elinor's voice sounded calm, even slightly bored.

"I had to take precautions, you understand. I had no other choice but to shoot the bulldog. That would be you, darling ... just before he ripped my throat open. I do hope that your wound is not serious. Please, forgive me if I made you suffer.

"There is one more thing you need to know. I decided it would be wise to use the services of *Wild Life Ltd* as you had already done. Perhaps you still remember the broken glass that cut your hand that night before you attacked me? I hope you have not forgotten the droplet of water. Concentrate on that droplet, dear; it is a very important item.

"*Wild Life* helped me and transformed me into a strain of virus, the HIV virus to be exact, dear. They wriggled in that droplet of water, the poor darlings and before the wound on your hand healed, I penetrated your bloodstream.

"Doctor Burrows informs me that the HIV virus does not reproduce itself for ten days after entering its host's body. Henry, I'm afraid you have already lost nine days. At this point, you have at your disposal no more than four hours. Within this limited period of time you will have to transfer all your property—companies, trusts, assets and stocks—into my name. I also require that you give me a written statement, confirmed by the signature of a notary, that you will divorce me. Otherwise, the HIV virus will begin to reproduce in your blood and the experts of *Wild Life* will not be able to transform me back into the loving woman that I am.

"If you choose not to carry out my request, you will have the consolation that I shall accompany you to the world beyond; I hope that you won't mind my being a virus causing AIDS, will you? Goodbye, dear."

Henry Cunningham remained immobile for more than a minute. The beads of perspiration trickled down his forehead, wetting the neat bandages. His hands reached for the beautiful woman; her face had almost entirely blanched. She recoiled, terrified.

"A notary! A notary! I need some paper!" Henry Cunningham started shouting. "Quick! Quick! Quick!"

"Goodbye, Henry Cunningham," said the magnificent Florence Hughes as she sashayed through the door, swaying her exquisite thighs.

"Flo! Flo! Please help me!"

Henry wept; there was nobody left in the room.

BAVARIAN STYLE

Any minute now, I expected that the man I was having dinner with would produce a letter typed on a sheet of yellow paper. I wasn't too happy about it, but I tried to enjoy my Hare with Chestnuts Bavarian Style, sipping at my glass of fabulous Chardonnays d'Oc. The guy who had asked me out was very attractive. His Chardonnay was excellent, his dark suit was immaculate, his blue eyes were interested in me and his name was Udo Fischgrund. He was the senior manager of the company which dealt in a wide range of French, American and German cosmetics of worldwide repute.

I'd eaten half of my Hare Bavarian Style, but the yellow letter I disliked with all my heart hadn't become a topic of our conversation. This made me feel uneasy and alert.

The reason why that letter gave me cold feet was, by all means, ludicrous. My mother was at the bottom of it all. She was a woman of character, that was all there was to it. If the old fair lady had something on her mind she was sure to get what she'd bargained for.

This sort of thing had happened to me quite a few times before, so I was well aware of the trap Mother had laid for me. She was good at making everybody around her suffer.

The turn the events would take as they followed the plan my mother had drafted always hit me hard. My admirer, the man expected to propose to me, at a certain point at dinner would produce a letter scrawled or typed on a yellow sheet of paper. That particular tinge of the yellow color gave me bitter headaches. It exuded smells of the drawer in which my mother stored her cosmetics. I had the feeling the paper had absorbed the memories of all the wrinkles she had concealed under thick layers of rouge. To put it mildly, the yellow paper smelled of problems that Mother hoped cosmetics could resolve. So when my prospective husband asked, "What is this?" showing me the yellow letter, I sensed I'd lose the battle one more time.

The yellow document was the letter in which Mrs. Schwarzmuller, my mother, had thrown light upon the some remarkable facts. The epistle read:

"Lieber Herr (Dear Sir),

I doubt you have the vaguest idea about the woman you intend to share your future with. She is my only daughter, Sir, therefore I feel responsible for you. It was me who brought her up doing my best to share with her the human values of our civilization. I put in quotes the noun "civilization" because my daughter and the civilized world are totally incompatible entities. In short, she is a liar. If she says she loves you, lieber Herr, this can only mean one thing: you are a very rich man. She is after your money, believe me.

She is bound to squander all your assets, all your hard earned savings, Sir. She will make you a beggar before you could say Jack Robinson. In short, my daughter is a spendthrift. I'll reiterate that statement in clear conscience in any court of law as the case may be.

I'd like to add she has lax morals. I've written those bitter words feeling utmost pain. You can understand that, I am her mother. I think I know what will happen to you; I have already lived through similar circumstances several times. Two other men before you, lieber Herr, were credulous enough to welcome her in their lives. Soon after that the poor guys, God bless their souls, came to me complaining of acute insomnia and lack of appetite. She'd cuckolded them. Her ex-boyfriends suffered nervous breakdowns. I, being a sensitive woman, wept silently and lived in constant dread of my high blood pressure. Therefore, I ask you to put an end to your relationship with my daughter. If you do not take my advice, you are sure to land in a psychiatric institution, and I, on my part, might as well meet my Maker as a result of being hypertonic. Alas, unfaithfulness is as indispensable to my daughter as is water to a fish.

At the end of the first month of your marriage, she will have fallen in love with another man. You are a sensitive guy—I can somehow feel that. Therefore, mein lieber Herr, run away on her if your future means something to you. Run for dear life while you are still able to wrench yourself from her grip.

I wish you good luck with all my heart. Please accept the assurances of my highest consideration.

Extremely worried about you,

Mrs. Elfriede Schwarzmuller,
Victoria Schwarzmuller's mother."

At that point, the guy who had already bought an engagement ring for me would stare at the yellow letter, rendered speechless.

More often than not my prospective husbands had asked me to a romantic candlelit dinner, the usual eight candles burning mystically, Vivaldi's *Spring,* a magic in the air. However, after the young man was halfway through my mother's epistle, his face would grow thin and long.

My first boyfriend read the yellow letter, gasping in astonishment as he looked at me,. His mother came to check what the matter was and in no time there were tears in her eyes. She pleaded with me to go away on my own accord. The poor woman hailed a taxi for me and sent me packing while my boyfriend sighed at the window, looking pitiful as I got into the taxi. My second boyfriend's father acted in a somewhat innovative way. His son had received my mother's letter, too. The text was identical, and it was only the date that was different. The father, having adopted a businesslike approach, informed me, "I make much more money than Friedrich, the son. I've been looking for a woman like you." Those words made the son start sobbing.

After that sad event, I made a pledge I'd have nothing to do with men who sobbed. So far, I had been as good as my word.

So far, Udo Fischgrund, the senior manager, had produced no yellow letter, and that fact, instead of pacifying my troubled thoughts, made me choke on my Hare with Chestnuts Bavarian Style. It sounded highly improbable that Mother had let my present admirer slip unobserved from her eagle's eye.

The yellow smell of an old drawer seemed to hover in the air above my head. Udo smiled at me, the candles burned romantically, Vivaldi's *Spring* was again a magic in the air, and I suspected a trap.

"Your mother is a marvelous woman," said the man I hoped against hope to grow old with.

Two weeks ago, Mother dropped insightful hints that I'd die all alone, an author of best selling memoirs replete with red hot love affairs. I didn't like that. Finally, Udo Fischgrund produced the yellow letter.

The moment of truth had come. This time, Mother had written the following:

"Lieber Herr (Dear Sir),
You are a fortunate man: you have met my daughter, a magnificent woman. I brought her up and I am proud of her. She is my creation, a flawless creation, sir.

65

Victoria would never lie to anyone even if her life depended on that. If she says she loves you it means that you are the love of her life and you will be the love of her life until she breathes her last. Loyalty is what describes best her character. Money is not of primary importance to her, however my statement should not be misunderstood: **she is not** a squanderer. On the contrary, sir! Victoria is the thriftiest young lady I know.

She will successfully accompany you along the way to stable financial prosperity.

My daughter's love for you will be your safe haven, now and for good. It is the thought of the harmony between you two that stabilizes my dangerously fluctuating blood pressure.

I feel that she can make you very happy.

Please, accept the assurances of my highest consideration.

Mrs. Elfriede Schwarzmuller, Victoria Schwarzmuller's mother."

P.S. Lieber Udo,

Thank you for sending me the high precision blood pressure/pulse measurement Eucerine device you and I talked about last month. I received it yesterday. Now I feel healthy, energetic and able to control my blood pressure under most untoward circumstances.

I simply adore the anti-cellulite apparatus you sent me for St. Valentine's Day! Could you believe the miraculous thing eliminated the abominable freckles on my hands that old age had given me? You have no idea how young I feel!

I was enchanted when yesterday you told me about the fibrinogen evaporator with which a lady can delete her wrinkles for good.

You are a serious scientist. I am proud of you!

Mit herzlichen Gruessen (All my best),
Elfriede

SLOWLY

There was something wrong with that room, he thought. The woman didn't even look at him.

He drank his wine slowly, trying not to stare at her. Her words were flat, and there was wine in their sounds that pressed his eyes against the table. She had invited him to her study, to the armchair beside the heavy tomes by Shakespeare and Schiller. The books were arranged in alphabetical order first and second, depending on the weight of the gilt on their jackets. He had visited her place several times. Now he hoped she'd speak about the snow that fell like wet rags from the scuffed sky. Last time she had given him the same armchair. He had been silent, she had not done anything, absolutely anything, just sat, staring tactlessly at his face, sipping at her wine that must have cost her husband a fortune.

"I thought I'd never get over it," the shards of her words whirred in his face. "I'd been saving my teacher's salaries. I had put aside all the money I took from the private lessons in that backwoods village. My student's parents paid me beans, tomatoes, eggs, rarely pennies. I collected the levs I got in my pillow."

It was difficult for him to place that refined woman beside a shabby pillow and a sweaty bundle of banknotes stuffed in it.

"I had saved up enough to buy a small house. Houses in the country are not expensive. The village was wild with howls of wolves in winter, with owls that lived in the linden tree in my landlady's backyard. Autumns came with mushrooms that sprouted up overnight in front of my threshold. I put up with the owls and wolves for my students' sake. Every night the growls of the wolf pack invaded my room instead of the newscast on the TV. I gave him all my money," her words tied an icy not around his wine. When they first met they made love, not kissing.

"He was important to me," the woman went on. "At that time I thought a human being is meant for another human. Banal, isn't it? I thought my life made sense only because I was born at the time when he picked mushrooms in my backyard and in the evenings sauntered with the owls to get to know the night. He was a poet. He dedicated his poems to me, to the river and the couple of owls. I believed my blood would disintegrate if I didn't see him. In the evenings, in the daytime, at nights I ran to his house, which was on the outskirts of the village. In fact all the houses were on the outskirts, the Town Hall and the mayor were the center.

My room was constantly in a mess, the floor and the cupboard were covered in dust and I wondered where the dust came from in that clean village. The road was dusty, yes. Perhaps time and clouds turned into dust."

He could not imagine the clutter in her room. Here even the shadows of the vases lay symmetrically on the Persian rug. The gold jewelry, the collection of sapphires and ancient swords glittered warmly, not a speck of clouds flitting over them.

"My salaries arrived with a delay of several months. I dreamt of the house I'd buy and he dreamt of becoming a great poet. I asked, "Isn't it enough that you have me?" It was not enough. He didn't have enough money to go and live in Sofia. I knew he'd become a great man. I couldn't live without his poems. I read them in the morning, in the evening, in the breaks at school. I gave him everything I had put aside. Folks paid me after harvest, after they sold their beans and the wheat.

"I'll give it back to you," he said and I knew he would. He had never lied to me. I believed his words the way I believed the clouds and the river that never ran dry in summer. He promised he'd come back during the spring term. Perhaps he'd make people's hearts explode, I hoped."

He wondered why she told him all that. He felt much better when her distant eyes did not linger on his face. Her words failed to bring him to the village where the river did not run dry. He couldn't care less what the poet had done. He knew him.

"It was a pile of tattered banknotes that the guys had got for their tomatoes and Indian corn, so their kids could analyze *Wild Stories* and other beautiful works of fiction which brought no one any good.

He went away, and I received a letter from him in which he explained how hard it was to find a rented flat in Sofia and how lonely he felt. There were two poems for me in the envelope. The howl of the wolves became my happy path and his poems illuminated the whole village that had only outskirts and no center at all. There was the Town Hall, too, with the mayor in it and, from time to time, his old friend from the armored troops.

That was the only letter from Nickolay I got. I glued it to the wall, beside the calendar. I must have taken leave of my senses, I guess. I circled in red ink the words in his letter every day I had no news from Nickolay. The red circles became so many I could build a bloody-soaked pyramid with them. After a couple of months that I spent in the company of owls, the folks from the neighboring villages dropped hints I had a screw loose.

They stopped sending their kids to me and I had no one to give private lessons to. One day I received a parcel, a magazine in which Nickolay's poems were published, plus an invitation card asking me to kindly attend Nickolay's wedding. The card explained Nickolay had married a Milla Kirova. It let me know where the wedding feast would take place: Bulgaria Restaurant.

Then I contracted anemia. I could not eat. The smell of food made throw up. I vomited when I saw the owls; I vomited when people talked to me. I vomited and not only my young students avoided me, their parents chose the opposite end of the village to get out of my way. It didn't matter to me. I obstinately went to school, to the only classroom where the students had lessons, but the kids were scared. They clumped together by the door and peeked inside the room together with the mayor and his fellow-soldier from the armored troops. Wolves howled from the blackboard. One day the mayor and his old friend dragged me out of the classroom and took me to the ambulance that usually arrived in the village when somebody had died. The mayor himself drove me to the county hospital in Radomir.

I don't remember how long I saw owls, wolves, the outskirts of the village, Nickolay's letter and the circles in red ink. I remember that I wrenched out the needle through which the doctors infused drugs into me to make me a human being again.

I trudged from the hospital to the village for a week, maybe two weeks. Lorries stopped and gave me a lift. I did what the drivers wanted, and I did things that the drivers could not think of. Every evening of that month sick with wet snow, I ate a piece of the magazine with his poems. The lorry driver did not understand I fed on poetry. He asked me if I was in my right mind, but it was not because of my right mind that he kept me on the passenger's seat. Not because of my right mind the lorry deviated from its usual route, turning to the nearby groves, to the driver's country shack where he gave me as a present to his cousins.

It was only natural I lost my job in the village with the owls and the only classroom. I lost the mushrooms and the mountain, I lost the howl of the wolves, but sometimes I can still hear it, especially when I drink from this wine, sir."

He avoided her eyes, cold like a screech of the owls she was talking about. Her face was a wolf's howl that bit the gilded jackets of the books.

"I didn't have any money, I didn't even have clothes. The sweaters I put on smelled of lorry drivers, of groves and cousins, but at least they did not smell of Nickolay. There was no village and no mayor of the armored troops in them."

She fell silent, her eyes pressing the collection of ancient swords. That woman's study was in fact a picture gallery and it constantly rained in her pictures. There were black and white drawings, and there was a collection of sapphires and gold that appeared black. Her study had nothing to do with the wayside groves, the drivers and the wolves in her mountain. Perhaps rains were different; some were for the books with gilded jackets, others remained in her cold eyes for good.

He could not understand why she gave him that expensive wine that probably cost as much as one of those houses with owls in the attics and mushrooms in the backyards. Maybe that bottle cost more than the whole village that had outskirts and a mayor, and no center at all.

"Your husband will be back soon," he told her, astonished that she remained unimpressed with his remark.

"No, Petar won't be back soon," she said. "You are a quiet man. It's my pleasure talking to you."

"First, I became Mr. Petar Savov's housekeeper. Imagine the chaos in the woods I was accustomed to, the notebooks, the sheets of paper, the dictionaries I've cluttered my desk and bed with. There were Nickolay's poems, too, glued to the chest of drawers, to the table and the mirror. My room had walls built of poetry, of owls and the moon. I never knew where my pens and my bag were. My head was Nickolay's words he had written for me, for my dry flowers in an empty plastic bottle.

In Mr. Savov's house all swords lay at a 45 degree angle to the base of the boxes. The brocade on the sofas is folded 12.5 centimeters from the floor.

I could cook scrambled eggs. I milked my landlady's cow and drank the milk from the bucket. I ate sorrels and bread when I was hungry in the breaks. I drank raw eggs and rain water. Mr. Savov adored French cuisine and hired a cook from Fevre-sur-Mere to train me. It was agony learning the names of the 127 spices the French cook had brought with him. Imagine me cooking a smoked duck with sugar beet, caramel sauce and raisins. I had boiled potatoes before, and that was all I had cooked. I had to arrange two inch spoon 8.6 centimeters from the oyster saucer and the three inch knife 2 centimeters from the spoon."

The wine from the ancient Bordeaux cellar scorched his throat. Her words were mad ducks in caramel sauce and raisins, and he could hear their wings flapping in his face.

"I can't imagine that," he said.

"Mr. Savov gave me the sack a number of times. I stayed in a garret owned by two Turkish women who sold second-hand clothes at the Housewife's Market. They let me spend the night under their roof because I taught them to speak Bulgarian. One of them told me, "Your eyes are great." She was not interested only in my eyes, but when she went on saying what else was great about me I left their place and strolled at midnight along the Housewife's Market. It was beautiful and quiet, no crush, no shoppers, the stalls like owls hovering over the sidewalks.

I visited an old lady and her cat that was almost as big as the woman. The front door of her apartment gaped open all the time like the Town Hall of that village. She walked with difficulty, gasping and choking, and when I entered her home she said she'd call down curses on me. I was not scared of curses. I had eaten so many pages of that poetry magazine and so many trucks had given me a lift from the hospital to the owls in the village. I learned the 129 spices of the French cuisine and I made Mr. Savov's bed every morning, leaving 12.5 centimeters of brocade visible from the floor.

I still don't know why Mr. Savov sent his bodyguard to bring me back to his house. Surely not because I glued dozens of pages of "Wild

Stories" all over the lumber room he had allowed me to move into. The letters on the pages reminded me of the kids I taught to read and write, of their parents who paid me tomatoes and hot peppers they plucked from their meager gardens. He did not bring me back to his house on account of the heap of second-hand jeans and T-shirts, which I had left behind.

The Turkish woman who said my eyes were great gave the clothes to me and asked me to recite *Visit Your Mother's Place* for her.

She cried for her mother's place, for the cherry trees covered with clouds of white blossoms, and her tears dripped onto my hand. She wanted to drink her tears from my hand, but I fled to the old lady and her cat.

The old lady stopped calling down curses on me. Once she gave me money to buy aspirin for her; she fought death with aspirin and hoped to win the game. I did not steal her money and when I came back from the pharmacy, instead of curses she gave me her full blessing. It could hardly bring me any good. Once she and I recited together Goethe's *Ruhe* and she sobbed. It was not because she was hungry or lonely. She felt her shadow flit beyond the Housewife's Market and no one but me would see death passing through the gaping front door of her apartment.

Mr. Savov's men dragged me from the Turkish women's garret, from the old lady's shadow and the desperate songs of her cat. They brought me back to the lumber room where the walls told the wild stories. In fact, the walls were the kids I taught in the only classroom of my life. When Savov asked me why I wasted my time on these scumbags from the Housewife's Market I lied to him, I said I wanted to become a nun.

Savov is a silent man like you, but he doesn't drink. He just sits in his armchair, intent, waiting, watching me set in order his spoons, his swords, his cigars. He threw out his fashion model for no apparent reason at all, maybe because the girl had set fire to my books in the lumber room. He didn't have to prove to me he was a man of genius, I knew he wasn't.

It was after his child was born, after I gave birth to Savov's son and the doctors said the baby was normal, that he stopped throwing me out of that lumber room. He forbade me to amble down to the Housewife's Market. I went there all the same. I hoped the old lady and I could recite *Ruhe* once again, but her shadow had already vanished beyond the

72

clouds and her apartment had a strong metal door. Her cat was nowhere in sight. The Turkish woman told me, "I'll give my mother's best golden coin. Please, stay with us."

Savov's son is a healthy lad and he proudly shows him off to his friends. I know all the spices of the French, the Bavarian and the Italian cuisine. I can make spaghetti with 21 different sauces. All brocade bedspreads in the mansion are exactly 12.5 centimeters from the floor.

Drink all your wine, please. Prepare yourself. That will make it easy on me. I hope my husband finds us. I don't see any reason why he should keep me here anymore. I have money — enough to buy the only classroom in that village.

He rose from the chair. She was a generous woman. She had left a bundle of banknotes for him in a saucer exactly 12.5 centimeters from her sapphire collection, just like the first time.

She looked at him and the glass of expensive wine in his hand shook.

"Nickolay sends you this," he said. His words sounded sharp, like ancient swords in the golden air of her books. "That's the money he owes you. He hired me to find you for him." The banknotes in his hand looked humped. There was wolf's howl in them. "Nickolay's looked for you."

The woman took a sip of her wine. Her hand as thin as the river that did not run dry in summer did not go for the money.

"He told me that after he sent you that magazine with his poems he could not write any more," the man said.

TIME TO MOW

"Heat," Lena murmured as she retreated into the shadow of the barn. She was afraid to stay in the sun. The meadows reeled before her eyes; the grass lay in the thick shimmering haze. The spring in Mitto's yard had almost run dry, but a little puddle of thin mud still glittered, narrow like an adder's eye. Frogs crept to the shallow water. Black, well-trodden earth was all over the place, groaning under the tires of tractors, hissing under the hooves of cows and horses, the black flinty grains of sand radiating heat like a burning stove.

How come the frogs touched the flaming earth with their gentle white bellies, Lena wondered. How did they manage to bring their spawn alive to the moisture? She had not seen their thirsty brown-green caravans sneak to Mitto's yard, but all the same, in the beginning of July, the puddle swarmed with tadpoles. They wriggled, pushing each other, noiseless in the tepid mud. At noon, usually a couple of small, black balls with tails baked on the sand, trying hard to zigzag back to the water, but remained in the heat, turning gradually into little tailed pieces of scorched leather. Children collected them and tied their tails on strings.

"Soon there will be no moisture at all," Lena thought. "What will happen to the tadpoles?" She imagined the sand tightening around their bellies, she saw them die, hot pieces of black wizened leather in the dry earth, neither frogs nor tadpoles any more.

Lena had to bring the scythes; it was July, time to mow the meadows. The grass had already shed its seeds. Lena was thirty-two. Ten years ago, on her birthday, when the meadows were ripe, her mother told her, "I hope you will bring some man to our place. We need him to mow the grass."

Lena did not bring anyone. She had grown accustomed to measuring the weedy ground by her quick steady steps. Many times, she, too, had participated in the mowing. It was a meadow full of sun and grass that hid the heat in its blades, and looked as though it might explode. Ten years had passed since she mowed for the first time. She had worked hard hoping to fall asleep the minute she lay in her bed. She did not want to dream about anything. The things she saw in her dreams scared her, they appeared so real at night. She could not talk to anyone about them for people would say she had a dirty mind.

"Heat," Lena whispered, shouldered the scythes, then hesitated for a moment, unwilling to go out. She imagined the three of them—her mother, her grandmother, and her—beginning to mow; the oldest woman slowly, apathetically, her mother mulishly, her hands blackened and tired, Lena angrily as if she bit into the thick impenetrable grass. The more they mowed, the broader sprawled the meadow before their eyes. The three of them had fought that dry, unyielding land, and they had dug out shallow canals to bring water to their garden. They struggled with the grass, but the meadow was enormous for their three pairs of hands. Every year the patch they managed to steal from the weeds and plant with tomatoes and onions grew narrower.

"Time to mow," her mother would whisper, and suddenly her white shoulders would appear younger. The wind pressed them impatiently and stumbled over her gently wrinkled neck.

Several consecutive years, when the clover was ripe in July, a strange man, Encho by name, used to come over to their place. They had eleven years of that strange man, who stayed with them for a fortnight. Every summer, he looked gloomier. The scythe on his shoulder appeared to be heavier as the heat at his feet mingled with his shadow, the grass asleep in neat fragrant heaps after the reddish patch of his neck.

"We have to pay him," her mother would say.

"I guess we have to," Lena's grandmother agreed, busy with a bottle of thick yellow brandy she prepared for him. Encho hardly talked to the old woman.

Every evening, her mother, dressed in a white blouse, failed to bring the brandy to the brown man as she went out barefoot at dusk. The stars put on white garments, too, and everything sparkled: the woman, the moon, and the stars in the hot breeze. In the morning, she came home pale, exhausted, unwilling to prepare the breakfast, and hid in the narrowest room of the house which had only one small window to the north.

Lena often took her mother's blouse to wash, and rubbed, and beat the white cloth until her fists hurt.

The brown man came at noon, bending slightly under the weight of the scythe. He worked hard, making the meadow ugly and naked, its greenish scalp of grass wallowing in the summer dust. Lena peeked at him from the kitchen. The afternoon heat made her feel uneasy, and she wanted to go somewhere far away. She stared at the half naked man, and all she saw were the dim outlines of the road vanishing in the distance.

A year ago, another man, an old man came to their place to help them mow the meadow. Lena's grandmother had asked him to their place. He was thinner than the handle of the scythe, tall, and withered. Lena's grandmother idled about him smiling radiantly, her decaying teeth shining like a yellow wreath in her gaping mouth. The old man tried hard not to fall asleep while her grandmother bombarded him with all sorts of questions. His hands trembled as he mowed, and the blade of the scythe would not cut the grass. Encho mowed alone, at the end of their yard. The two men never talked.

The minute the old man remained alone, he fell asleep, clutching the handle. His face and the worm-eaten wood of the same whitish color melted in the heat of July. Soon after he went home, they received his obituary notice.

The awkward smile vanished from her grandmother's face for good, but the old woman could not break her habit of preparing the bottle of yellow brandy. Weeks on end it waited in the cupboard ready for a helper. In the evening, when the three of them had dinner, Lena's grandmother often remarked, "We can pay Encho with it."

Lena realized she had learned to mow evenly and smoothly, and she had imperceptibly turned from a girl into a woman, but she longed to leave the grass green and thin in the night, and watch the wind make love to the blades. She wanted to feel the evening sleep on their soft meadow. She hoped that one day she'd go out barefoot in the twilight and, like her mother, would return in the morning, tired, uneasy, to sleep in the narrow room with the small window to the north.

"The tadpoles," she heard herself mutter, angry with the endless month of July. She hated the baked land, the purple sun, which tightened the knot around the puddle in Mitto's yard. The gray-tailed balls would never become frogs. She didn't know why she loved them. Day in day, day out, she went to watch how much water had remained in the puddle.

Her evenings dissolved into nothing, the ceaseless croon of the crickets spied on her blood, the fragrance of the oak door to their big yard made her hot and jumpy. No one came in through that door.

One evening, she went to Mitto's puddle and quickly, stealthily, shoveled mud and tadpoles into a bucket. There were no passers-by at that time, she knew, but casual shadows made her bend over the black well trodden earth.

The river between the two hills had run dry and had left a scar of salt on the rocks. Only one little spring that had never surrendered to the heat was still alive. Lena had to find it and make its cool golden water a home for the frogs. She trudged through the baked mown field, hoping she'd drop with fatigue in the evening and the obscene dreams would not bother her. But even in the daytime, they were everywhere—in her steps, in the dust, in the thick hot air.

This year, they still had not mown their meadow. It was the only patch of land in the village, still beautifully overgrown with whispering grass. Lena felt as though her blood was pushing to escape from her. It did not want to stay where it was.

She had to work, had to mow, to run, or to shovel more mud from the puddle into the bucket. She grabbed the scythe, thinking of the tadpoles she had helped to become frogs. She worked and worked, brandishing the scythe in wide semicircles, her hands cracking, the sky above her head reeling, blending with the fence into a sticky mess. Her mother and her grandmother stood under the shade of the eaves staring at the tall thin figure waist-deep in the hot grass.

"She's like you," her grandmother whispered to her mother.

"Like us," Lena's mother said.

They were tall women, tough and unfriendly. The old house they lived in, meticulously whitewashed, with heavy grey tiles, looked like its owners—the narrow long windows resembled tightly drawn lips that never whimpered. The roof pressed the old bricks and walls that wanted to fly up to the sky just like the three women thought the village was too small for them.

Her mother and her grandmother worked in a shirt factory in the nearby town. In the morning, they went out together, silent, taking equal steps, dressed in the same blouses. At lunch, they ate the same food that

Lena prepared for them, wrapped in a bundle. They did not speak behind the heaps of ready collars that towered like an avalanche in front of them. They took their annual leave when it was time to mow the meadow. That's when Lena saw them smile, age slipping down their faces like grains of sand. Although there was no strange man at home, they opened the drawers of the chests and took out their new dresses. They mowed slowly, unevenly, their bodies young again. After the mowing was over and the meadow sprawled naked and ugly, their faces looked wrinkled.

Lena got into the family habit of doing that as well. She put on her Sunday best as she mowed. She carried the bucket with the tadpoles to the spring, her best dress on. She used to work in the kindergarten, but there was no kindergarten any more. One child and she, the only teacher, remained in the spacious building. Lena loved that little girl and talking to the child, she could hear the secret noises of her endless childhood, and could smell the fragrance of her mother's quiet old house.

Lena went once more to the spring in the hills, her bucket full of wriggling tadpoles. On her way home, she saw a stranger. He did not look old. The heat trembled at his sandals as he walked quietly, like the shadow of a bird, along the arid hills, their rocks bristling in the dusk. Nothing happened. He saw her, and that was all.

A week passed. She saw him once more as he got off the bus in the center of the village. He had tied the blade of his scythe to its handle, his dirty flannel shirt almost colorless, and his legs dusty. She froze in her tracks, her eyes intent on him.

When his back became almost invisible, Lena ran after him. She had noticed he walked with a limp, she had seen the long red scar creeping to the knee of his right leg. She followed him to a haystack and watched as he shaved using an iron can, his whiskers bushy and tousled. She watched on as he took a bath in a wooden tub, and she felt ashamed of herself.

"He's driving you out of your mind," her mother said in the evening as she cut the bread for dinner. She spoke slowly and quietly, but Lena and her grandmother knew her voice could be stronger than the heat.

"Forget about him," her grandmother nodded. "He is a thief, and he's just got out of prison in Pernik."

79

The three women kept quiet, eating their supper. There was lemonade, too, and before her grandmother poured it out into the cups, her mother said, "That's a shame."

Lena did not look her in the eye. She coughed, then said huskily as if her tongue rasped the stubble of the meadow, "I'll go to see him." She knew that the stranger had been mowing Patresh hill, so she ran off down the street, the dry steep field a grotesque kite beneath her feet, her best dress hanging loosely on her hot dusty back. She ran and ran, and the afternoon was a frightened bell that rang in her shallow breath.

She stalked the man's shadow and watched fascinated by his scythe, by his legs, by his naked shoulders. This could not go on forever.

"Hey."

He was taken aback. She stood silent and watched him.

"What do you want?" he finally asked.

Lena liked his voice. It was as clear and deep as a mountain lake. She was ashamed to stare at the red scar on his right leg. She knew it started from his waist. Suddenly, she was afraid. She was gaping at him, and her face twitched.

"I want you to come over and mow at our place," she said.

It was difficult to breathe in the scorching afternoon air, but she had to go on.

"Come to mow our meadow. I'll pay you."

On the following day, the man came to their immaculately whitewashed house, his face unshaven, his dirty shirt unbuttoned. Her mother and her grandmother had already taken their scythes and were mowing, thin translucent laths in the furnace of July. They did not pay any attention to the stranger, their eyes intent on Lena, their faces gray and closed.

The man walked slowly past them; he did not look at them, did not bother to stop, and say, "How do you do."

Lena was anxious to hear him talk, to peek at the man under the slippery surface of the words, but he was silent.

Why did you remain alone? Lena asked her mother in her thoughts. How come our house is always empty? She did not know her father. When Lena was a little girl, she had heard her grandmother mention a son-in-law. All Lena knew about him was his name, Kamen, and that her mother, still big with child, had collected her husband's clothes in a neat bundle and left them at the oak door. There had been some other woman, but her grandmother never talked about her.

Thirty years, that door had been locked, and no Kamen was allowed to enter their home. Her mother spent her nights waiting for the old screeching bus, for her short July with Encho. Lena tried to imagine Encho kissing her mother's thin lips. It seemed impossible.

One evening, Lena hid in the cellar and there, in the dark, she put on a white blouse. She didn't want to meet her mother, so she went out the back door and jumped over the fence. Suddenly, the night put on a white gown and the grass turned white.

The stranger had fastened the blade of the scythe.

"What do you want?" he said over his shoulder.

She watched his hands. The red scar on his leg was now invisible. His body looked thin and dark, and her eyes hurt.

"Well?" the man said facing her.

"I … I brought you brandy," Lena stammered. The bottle was alive and hot in her hand. The man took it and had a long drink. Then he put the bottle on the ground, lifted his scythe, and walked away, his steps echoing, his scythe dark and dumb.

She stared, helpless. It seemed she could hear the frogs croak; perhaps her tadpoles had grown up in the cool July spring.

She shuddered, then slowly unbuttoned her white blouse, and her naked skin shimmered like the moon. The leaves of the walnut trees were crumpled brittle funnels of green in the red hot dusk. A soft voice crept out of the meadow and touched Lena's scrawny shadow.

"It can happen to anyone," her mother was saying.

Her grandmother was there, too, in the room with the window to the north, staring.

Lena did not know where her grandmother's husband was. She had always known her as a tall, proud woman, dark-eyed, silent.

In her childhood, her mother and her grandmother would keep silent in the kitchen. They would not fight; they would just sit at table and eat separately for days, for months. The rustle of slippers, touching the floor, was the only sound in the rooms as if there lived slippers, not women. But everything was different when their happy July came.

That night Lena hated them. The heat set the earth on fire, the bell of darkness rang, and Lena did not prepare the bundle with breakfast for them. When the moon fell behind the chimney of their house, and the sky was quiet, she put her white blouse once more. She knew where the stranger was; he slept in the haystack in their big yard. He heard the noise of her steps, but did not react, his back a dark arch, bent over his scythe. She waited.

"What do you want?" he asked.

"You know what I want." She had prepared the answer long time ago.

"That's why you follow me, eh?"

"Yes."

The unshaved man fastened his bundle slowly. The blade of his scythe twinkled.

"It will be expensive," he said at last.

The heat melted Lena's eyelids. The night whirled and hit her red hot cheeks.

"I ... I'll pay.

In the morning, Lena was up as early as usual, preparing their breakfast.

"What happened?" her mother asked.

Lena gave no answer. In a minute, her grandmother saw her waist deep in the grass, clutching the scythe like a banner. The strange man came, stood facing Lena and began to work. They did not talk, did not look at each. They mowed like mad, silent, deaf to the shouts of the frogs high up in the spring. In the evening Lena ate her supper and slipped on her white blouse.

"Maybe he is a bad man," her grandmother ventured.

"He is a bad man," Lena said.

After that, nobody discussed him any more as though the women did not hear the swish of his scythe and did not see him drink water from the demi-john Lena left for him at the oak door. At last, he mowed the whole meadow. The hay lay motionless and fragrant, kissing the summer for the last time.

Lena's mother knew her daughter kept the money she had saved in a purse under her pillow. One day she checked it and froze. The money was no longer there.

"Think of the years you worked for it," she shouted to her daughter. "Don't give him anything ....you are crazy."

Lena did not say anything. Bent to the ground, numb, she clutched the money, all rumpled banknotes she had been paid in the kindergarten. She looked thinner and darker when she came home, her most beautiful dress hanging on her, her shoulders bent, drooping. That night Lena slept in the narrow room with the small window to the north for the first time. The next day the frogs were silent.

That day, a black cloud appeared in the sky. That day, it rained for the first time since the beginning of the summer. It was a downpour. Within an hour, the meadow turned into a lake. The fresh hay swam on its surface. The lashing rain soaked every single blade of grass. The three women had waited the whole year for that hay to get ripe. Now it whirled, jumped, and floundered like a shattered fleet of a thousand boats in the flood. Their hay was ruined.

No, it still was not.

The women tried to catch the blades of grass, to stop them, to save them. They ran after them, they waded waist-deep through the muddy water to guard them. They wanted their hay. They had hoped for it.

It was quiet in the evening. It rained no more. The sunset had a white blouse on as it brought back the voices of the frogs and the heat. The meadow lay in a wet silent mess, a waste of wet fragrant grass, a hot lost summer.

The three women got frightened. They looked and looked, dumbstruck.

"Come on," Lena's mother said.

Her grandmother brought out a big rectangular canvas from the barn, and the three of them began to heap the wet hay on it. They had to drag the canvas to the center of the village. There the square was of hot black asphalt. They had to scatter the hay in a thin layer there and let it dry off in the sun. They had to be patient. They had to endure. They had three pairs of hands. There were three miles to the square. They had to drag the canvas hundreds of times to the black patch of asphalt, to the sun, to safety. They had to drag it today, tomorrow, the day after tomorrow, that old canvas heavy with their ripe wet hay.

A man appeared on the road as they trudged the last mile to the square in the hot black dust. He had been waiting in the shadow of a walnut tree, dressed in a dirty flannel shirt, and a big red scar crept to the knee of his right leg. Lena saw him and averted her eyes from his face. Her mother and her grandmother did not look at him at all.

"Wait," the stranger said.

Lena tugged at the canvas and hurried forward.

"Get out of the way," her mother shouted.

"Lena, wait!"

The stranger grabbed the canvas then stretched out his right hand. A little roll of banknotes, frayed and crumpled, lay there. The man let the money fall into the pocket of Lena's old dress. He gave the heap of hay on the rough cloth a sharp pull and dragged it on by himself.

"I don't want your money, Lena," he said. "And I won't go away."

His voice, deep as a mountain lake, deafened the trumpets of the frogs.

NIKOLA AND THE CROCUSES

He could not look at the dog's eyes, light brown, like the sky before it started to rain. "Come on," Vassil said. The dog slowly followed him and climbed up on the backseat of the bone-shaker. Jivil was a peculiar mutt, yellowish-orange, like a crocus, but so feeble and aged that could hardly stand in front of his kennel. Jivil used to be a good guard of Vassil's house, but there was no life in the old dog anymore. When thieves once stole some instruments from the backyard, Vassil brought a new dog; white with brown and black spots on his back. There were no crocuses and no rains in him; the newcomer had sharp teeth, malice and youth and no burglar could lift anything from the backyard.

"Come on," Vassil repeated.

Vassil's car was a ramshackle Ford, third or fourth hand. He hated it when his friends saw him drive it. He imagined he looked like the old Jivil, his fur thinning at the back, rains in eyes, death stalking behind the clouds.

Vassil was forty-seven when his wife gave birth to a third child, a boy, after his two daughters had grown and had children of their own. The boy, a dot of a child with red hair, was called Nikola after his mother, Nika. While Nika did the housework, the boy and Jivil talked above the dog's empty bowl, a black eye, staring angrily at the sky.

The old Ford, which lacked any enthusiasm whatsoever, whirred and wheezed to the forest. Vassil knew he had to go a long way—not only to the village of Bosnek, but much further, behind the springs of the Struma River, into the wilderness where even wolves would lose their way. The man and the Ford plodded on, the dog barked at the road from time to time. "Shut up, Jivil," Vassil muttered. Perhaps Jivil was deceiving himself that his master was again taking him hunting despite his scuffed coat where his fur had fallen off. The dog constantly raised his nose to the windshield.

Vassil had risen early in the morning on purpose so Nikola could not see him.

Nikola was a quiet comma which separated the days of Vassil's life and made his home complete and alive. Even Vassil's back, that he had injured in Italy, did not hurt so much when Nikola was around. There was no place in the world where his thought could go if Nikola was not there.

There were dozens and dozens of holes in front of his Ford. Not a road but a guillotine for the poor car, which positively had driven more interesting folks in its heyday: Italians, and then some Turks from whom Vassil bought it. The guys just happened to pass through Pernik and were grateful they finally got rid of their rusty rattle-trap.

Vassil was a teacher in Bulgarian literature but there were not enough students in town, so he taught at the school for mentally retarded children. His students had difficulties remembering things. His wife was a teacher in physics, but there were no vacancies so she made tapestry cushions and prepared to go and work at a hotel in Greece. Vassil could not feed an old dog at home. He could not leave him to starve either and he had no bread for two dogs

The road before Vassil vanished altogether, then the track disappeared and only the hill was left. "Come on," Vassil told the dog, but even before he had finished speaking, the orange pelt was jumping through the bushes. Vassil took out a plastic bag. There were bones and stale bread that he and his wife had been collecting for a week. Vassil had added a piece of cheap sausage. He had hidden it yesterday night from his dinner. He could do that much for Jivil.

He and his wife had carefully taken away the cubes of bacon from the sausage for Nikola. One never knew what sort of bacon they put in that cheap sausage. Vassil emptied the plastic bag with the bones and the shriveled piece of cheap sausage. The dog looked at him gratefully and bayed deeply, the way he did when Nikola took him for a walk to the hill. That hill was the end of the town of Pernik and the beginning of the disused colliery in which there were no coals. There were only rusty rails and old goods wagons in which snakes and spiders bred. The boy and the dog went about the deep ruts and Vassil was worried sick they could collapse in some old shaft.

"Eat this," he said to the dog. When Jivil licked his hand the man did not pat him on the head as usual. He withdrew guiltily, made for the car without turning back, started the engine and drove along the dirt road, through the holes, each one a grave for the ancient bone-shaker the Turks had gotten rid of.

The dog looked around confused, left the bones, and forgot even the shriveled piece of cheap sausage, which Vassil had kept for him from his dinner. His barking—deep, long and loud—mixed with the autumn leaves. Vassil could hear it, but didn't turn back for he didn't want to see the dog's back with the fur falling off, as orange as a crocus. He could not look at the eyes in which it constantly rained and death waited for the last autumn day.

The dog ran after the car. Finally he lost the game, yet made it to the asphalt road, crouched down beside it and set up a quiet deep-toned howl. Vassil drove quickly, as quickly as his old tub of a car could. He hated the rear view mirror although now it did not reflect the dog, but the roofs of the village of Bosnek. Vassil kept on seeing rain although it had stopped raining. It had stopped raining long ago. He parked his car in front of the school for mentally retarded children where the students studied very slowly. He was on duty during the night. He was in charge of all these kids, but he was not sure he could teach them any good at all.

In the afternoon he went home, to his house with which the town of Pernik ended and the empty colliery began. The railroad reached almost to the door to his backyard and abruptly ended there. On the curb, in front of the house, Nikola, the red-haired comma that separated into two all sentences in Vassil's heart, waited. Although it was autumn, his son sat on the stone and played with the frayed leash on which they kept Jivil. The boy had put half a piece of the cheap sausage in the black dog's bowl—an old piece of sausage, from which someone had carefully taken away all cubes of bacon. Nikola stood up from the curb—a mite, a little round stone, hurled near the house.

"Where is the—" he began, but his father cut him short.

"Listen, I am in a hurry. I have to help your mother."

The red-haired boy bent his head, a reddish kite that had by chance tumbled in their backyard. He rolled the leash into a ball and thrust it under his shirt.

At noon the boy fell sick. His mother left the tapestry cushions she was weaving. His grandmother, a small woman who lived in the neighboring borough and smiled easily, came. She brought honey and dried linden blossoms to kill the high temperature. The boy didn't say anything, just listened to her, as quiet as a crocus in his bed in the kitchen where it as warm. He easily swallowed the pills his mother gave him. On the following day the rain stopped, the wind came from the empty colliery smelling of old wagons and spiders, the street behind the window was full of autumn. The boy was again running a temperature and the doctor made up his mind to put him on antibiotics.

Vassil came back from school. The children there, although they had difficulties remembering and studying things, had made greeting cards for their teacher's red-haired boy. There were smiling kids in these cards and a couple of scribbled words, "Get well, Nicko."

Nikola, too small for his heavy grand name, lay in his bed in the warm kitchen and spoke to the TV that was on, or perhaps he was talking in his sleep. Vassil brought him another dog—a brownish-black thing that he kept on Jivil's leash. The boy tried hard to smile and gave up somewhere halfway through it. His mother sat by his side with a bottle of medicine and other pills.

It was cold and rainy, the red roofs of the houses thawed in the clouds, the wind hid somewhere and Vassil didn't know what else he could bring his son. It was quiet and gray and his boy probably lay in his bed in the kitchen. Vassil was walking slowly toward the end of Pernik, to the hill from which the autumn was to go away. It was impossibly quiet. The railroad of the colliery ended abruptly in this street, and his backyard began. If only Jivil could come back, but he had driven him far from here, too far. Even the Struma River was not there. There were no springs either, only wilderness. He'd do everything for his boy. There was nothing to be done. Vassil didn't feel like looking up. When he finally did, he couldn't believe his eyes.

Crouched by the curb, a boy and a dog sat side by side on the stone: Jivil and Nikola, both of them yellowish-red, the kid small, his hair very short, the dog's fur falling off from his back, two crocuses that had unexpectedly grown by the railroad of the colliery.

SHE

Yak had been teaching me to play the clarinet. I didn't like him and I didn't hide it.

Then the black Thursday came. "You are dumb," he said. "You are as stupid as my old shoe. You learn slowly. You are no good."

I ran to the biggest walnut tree, and I climbed it like a lizard. I perched amidst the branches and I started playing my clarinet. I didn't care about melodies, I played what I saw, I played the heat that made the grass burn. I played loud and strong to spite Yak. I played in the cellar in which Yak locked me. I roared at the top of my lungs, and I screamed in that dark cellar and spite him I did.

"You are dumb," he said me. "You are the dumbest thing I've ever met. I won't sign a document that you learned to play the clarinet with me. Then you'll go hungry like a dog."

"Are you sure?" I asked. I grabbed the clarinet and I climbed that big walnut tree. The clouds were my brothers there. I was as free as the sun in that tree. Yak said the tune I played was dirt, and that my clarinet wailed like a dying bitch.

And there was that Kika girl. She sneaked near the walnut tree when I played, and sat in the shadow as quietly as if she was dead. She listened. In the beginning, I thought she pretended she liked it. Perhaps she's trying to trick me into climbing down, I thought.

"I don't like you, Kika," I told her. "I don't like you at all. You are not pretty enough for me." She went away but after a couple of days I saw her sneak back. She stood in the heat listening.

"So Kika's your girlfriend," my master Yak told me. "Why am I not surprised? She is plain. My dog is more beautiful than her."

Maybe it was on account of those words I stopped telling Kika to go away.

"Okay, Kika," I said. "You may listen as long as you want."

And I played the clarinet. I played because it was hot, and I played because the land was as dry as the bones of a dead man and even the thorns in it were gloomy like a grave. I played because the dust covered all houses, and it covered the sky, too. Yak wanted to teach me play in his dark cellar where I couldn't feel the day, the wind and the heat.

"If you don't practice you won't eat at lunch and you will not eat at dinner," he threatened. I didn't practice just to spite him. I tried to burn everything that could burn in his damned cellar. I burned his old shoes and his clothes. He kept the door locked.

It was Kika who brought me some stale bread and some water, and it was Kika who said, "Could you play for me, please. I'll listen and it will be easier for you."

"You think you're so important that should play for you?" I said. "Go away." But when she was gone I knew I'd been mean, and although she was gone I played for her. I played, the smoke of Yak's smoldering shoes making my eyelids twitch.

Then Kika knocked at the little window of the cellar. I was grateful she'd come.

"Thank you for playing for me," she said.

"I didn't play for you."

"Well," she said. "It was beautiful all the same."

"Don't lie to me," I told her. I knew I was mean. "I don't care for you."

"I understand," she said. "I love what you play. I see the stars at noon and I see snow in summer. I'll stay in the shadow. I won't be in your way. I've never heard such tunes before."

"Shut up," I said and she shut up, and I saw her go away.

Later on, the poplar trees cast deep shadows and I thought, She's there, listening. I played something silly, then something light like a kite that crawled up the sky, like a green grasshopper that jumped in the grass, and I hoped she was in the shadow listening to me.

"You idiot," Yak told me. "A petticoat turned your head. But you know what? I paid her to come and bring you bread. I paid her to say your music was good." He looked at me and sniggered. "Kika doesn't know a wolf's howling from music. She'd say anything for a dime."

The following day I climbed that walnut tree and I played my clarinet. Kika sneaked closer, I could hear her steps but I couldn't see her, she was in the shadow. It was warm and it was late in the evening. She'd turned the shadow into a living thing that had eyes and ears, and I kind of liked it. I had never paid attention to shadows before. When Kika was under the walnut tree everything was different.

"Kika," I called out. She pushed her way out of the branches. "Kika, is it true Yak paid you to come and tell me my music was beautiful?"

"Yes, he did," she said. "But I said that because it was really beautiful."

"Yak says you are as ugly as his dog," I said. She was quiet, and she was small. I had to punish her; she had taken money from Yak. "I think you are no prettier than his dog, too," I said. She winced, and she looked smaller in the scorching heat. She turned her back to me, a narrow patch of faded cotton dress.

Yak came to me and said, "Do you want to know why I paid her to lie about your music?"

I didn't answer him, I knew. He wanted to make me the laughingstock of the village. The plain stretched before me dry like rust, the sky was rust too, blue and sharp. I couldn't look at it.

"I paid Kika to fawn on you because you make strange tunes," he said. "I copy them. They are no good, of course, but you can't pay me, so I copy your tunes. I repeat, they all are rotten, but at least I take something from you."

"Oh," I said. "You copy my tunes, eh? You grab my leftovers. Like a stray dog. Like a worm that eats dog's shit," I said, looking him in the eye. "Good for you, Yak."

His turned red. Spit flew out of his mouth.

"I never thought you were good with the clarinet," I said. "But I never thought you were as low as a shit eating worm either."

"You freak!" he shouted. His face was red like the meat of a skinned cow, the blood pumping in it, and shame pumping in it, too.

He grabbed stones and hurled them at me.

"I'll never sign any certificate for you," he said waving his hands at me. "You'll never see any certificate of a musician. You'll go hungry like a beggar!"

"You won't give me a certificate. So what? I spit on your certificate," I told him. It felt good watching his blood shoot up his face. "Do you want to see my certificate, Yak? Do you want to see it now?"

He dropped the stones and stared, his mouth gaping. I lifted the old clarinet and brandished it in his face.

"This is it, Yak. Look at it well. Look at it carefully and put it into your head that I don't care 'bout your certificate, you old worm."

He bent to grab something from the ground.

"If you touch another stone, Yak, I'll break your neck," I screeched.

He shook from head to foot, he reached out his hand and shook again, but he didn't dare to take another stone.

"That's much better," I said. "Mark my words, Yak. In a year I'll be rich. All guys in the mountain and all guys in the valley will respect my name. You'll be my servant, Yak. You'll wash my feet and you'll drink the water with which you've washed them. I won't force you to drink that water. You'll drink it of your own accord because I'll pay you."

His whole body shook.

"You rat!" he hissed. "You mongrel!"

It was hot and the wind was sharp, the mountain was bare, a wasteland of crags and burning red sand. His face was dark and his gray hair looked like a heap of dust. He didn't dare to say another word. He didn't dare to take a step towards me. I had never thought it would be so easy.

Then suddenly the night began singing. The darkness was thick and heavy and it felt good listening to the song. That was one of my tunes, one that my mother used to sing to me when I was a kid. It was a song I played on my clarinet. I recognized the voice and I wondered why I hadn't noticed how powerful and clear it was. It was a great voice.

"This is your bitch," Yak croaked. "She's like you."

It was Kika who had made the night sing.

"She is a bitch, but she's not my bitch," I said.

I didn't look at him anymore. I didn't listen to Kika who went on singing, I played on my clarinet. I played and there was fear in the clarinet that I wouldn't get a certificate, and there were hands rolling into fists in the tune, because I wanted to crush somebody like a nut, to beat him black and blue, to hit and clout him until he breathed his last. I was angry she sang my mother's song, and the clarinet poured my anger like a hailstorm. Then in the morning, I played on the village square for money.

My father came and said he was ashamed of me.

"You don't have a certificate," he said. "They won't take you in any band and you have to know I can't feed you."

"I don't want you to feed me," I said.

I didn't want to listen to him so I played on. My two older brothers came and threw some coins at my feet, small change that made me angry. Other people passed and they, too, tossed small change into my cap. Then my mother passed by.

"You play well son," she said and smiled. "Here take this," she left a bottle at my feet. "I didn't believe that my son could play so well."

She was small and gray, and I wanted to kiss her, and I wanted to make big money and give it all to her. I hated it when she got up in the middle of the night to bake bread for us.

Then she was gone.

Girls came and smiled at me. Kika came.

"Eat," she said and left a bag by the bottle of milk Mother had given me. "Eat while it's still warm."

I drank the soup she'd made and I played on. I played all day long, I played until midnight and the money I had collected was not enough to buy half a loaf of bread. I was hungry like a dog. On the following day, I played in the square again. Nobody gave me money, my mother passed again, gray and small.

"You play beautifully son," she said, and this time she didn't smile. Her face looked tired, and I knew she'd got up in the middle of the night to wash our pants and undershirts. I hated myself. I couldn't give her any money, I couldn't give her anything, and I saw how deep the wrinkles around her eyes were.

Then Kika came and brought me bread and a jar of thin soup. It was bean soup, I still remember it. I drank it in front of her and I guzzled the bread.

"Bring me more bread," I told her.

She opened her old worn bag and gave me another little piece. I ate it and I didn't say 'thank you'. I was so angry I hadn't made any money. It meant my tunes were no good. It meant my tunes were all rotten.

"Your tunes are beautiful," Kika said. "The people have nothing, that's why they don't give you money."

"Go away," I told her.

She didn't go away. She saw everything. She saw Yak's servants. They were seven or eight strong guys. She saw they kicked me and they stepped on my chest. She saw my blood mix with the dust and the cold red sand. She was the only one who tied to stop them, one of them kicked her and then I didn't see her any more.

That was how it all started. First, I caught the one who'd kicked Kika. I broke his nose I made him drink his own blood. I had planned to do exactly the same thing with the second guy I caught, but he said, "Don't kill me. I pay you."

I beat up a guy within a couple of minutes, and I made more money than my father and my four brothers earned for a month. Then I caught another guy from the group, I beat him and he paid me not to kill him. I made good money. I traced and caught all the seven of them, and I caught Yak. He offered me all his clarinets, an accordion and a bagpipe.

"You didn't give me a musician's certificate," I told him. "Why should I take your clarinets now?"

I broke his nose and his blood mixed with the red sand and the frozen dirt.

Then, once again, I heard that clear powerful voice singing in the shadow. Kika. No one else had a voice like that. The wind and the night hummed with her, and I thought the summer came back. That was the song my mother used to sing to me when I was a kid. It was beautiful, and sad, and I thought of my old clarinet I had thrown under my bed. I remembered I had other noses to break, I remembered I made more money for an hour then my brothers did for a month.

"Shut up!" I screamed to the shadow that sang. "Shut up, bitch."

I wished she hadn't stopped singing. I wished her rich voice remained with me and I could play the clarinet again. Suddenly the night was silent. Kika was gone.

Now I am rich. Now I have money to burn.

My mother died.

"I don't want money from a murderer," she spoke to me from her deathbed. "Go away and don't come back here."

I made her a rich grave with a marble monument. I couldn't forget the song she sang to me when I was a kid. It was in the wine I drank, and it was in the shabby streets of the village.

I'd had many women, and I had a wife. She gave birth to three sons. The youngest one found my old clarinet and tried to play on it and I hit him so hard I broke two of his fingers.

Yak is my servant now. He washes my feet every evening. Once in a while he drinks the water with which he's just washed them because I pay him generously. I have many servants, who want to wash my feet, but I allow only Yak to do that, and I let only Yak eat the food I've left in my plates. He's become very fat. One day I heard him play the clarinet and I broke his nose again. It was summer and his blood mixed with the dust and the red sand. My wife can't sing. She used to dance but now she's fat and she doesn't dance any more.

I have money to burn, I wallow in money. My sons have the best clothes and the best food. I am a rich and happy man. I have everything I want.

One night I heard the shadow sing. The voice was clear and strong, and so huge I couldn't breathe. Then there was a clarinet playing. The guy who played it was no good. The miserable tune reeled and stammered, the melody wobbled and hobbled all over the place. Then the voice started again, more scorching than the heat, more powerful than the wind, bigger than my money, bigger than my three sons and my fat wife. I knew the voice.

Everyone in these parts knew what happened to the guy who dared play the clarinet. I kept nine sacks of black dust ready to absorb the blood of that stupid son of a bitch. I hated the idiots who played the clarinet. I hated their guts.

My servants ran toward the shadow that had burst into song. Yak was the first to reach it. I knew this song. It was not the one my mother used to sing to me to lull me to sleep. It was the tune I played when I climbed the old walnut and I saw the bare mountain ridge. No trees, no lizards, no grass, only sharp stones used to rumble in that tune. I couldn't breathe. It was enormous, it was magnificent, that rumbling song, it was big and it hit me hard.

I ran to the shadow and I saw her.

"Kika!" I called out.

I saw her dress in the dim light of the lanterns. It was cheap. Her face was small and tired. There was a boy by her side, a little mite. Under the bright torches, his trousers looked old and creased, and his shirt had many patches on it. The kid was playing the clarinet. Slowly, jerkily, looking for the right sound that came with difficulty, the boy played on. He lost the tune, found it again, then there was no tune at all—just blind silence—like a puppy that was unsure which way to go.

"Take your bastard and go away," Yak screamed at the woman.

I couldn't move. The tune that was bigger than the bare mountain ridge was still in my ears. The uncertain sounds the boy produced were in my ears.

Yak pushed the woman. Under the lanterns, the boy looked smaller than his clarinet.

"Go away!" Yak shouted and pushed the boy.

I hit Yak hard. I hit him so hard that suddenly the tune and the clarinet were silent. I listened and listened. The song that was bigger than the mountain was gone.

TOSSING

The lakes in Josaphat Park in Brussels were heavy with pale, sickly water lilies. The benches looked forlorn and moldy. Thick crowds of ravens hung above the trash cans, glum birds, bigger than the clouds. It rained constantly, day and night. Josaphat was the centre of the Arab neighborhood in Brussels. Here the women walked slowly, majestically. Heavy women wrapped up in brown veils, followed by clusters of children, big and small. The braver boys fed the ravens, the girls led their mothers by the hand diligently, dutifully, talking to each other in beautiful, soft voices. I watched them every day as I practiced speaking French in Chez Albert, the cheapest pub in the park.

Albert, the owner of the place, asked me to make Bulgarian salads for his customers, all of them pensioners who lived in the imposing building which he also owned,, La Maison Communale, across the street,. The old gentlemen believed it rained esspecially for them. Each would tell me maybe this was the last rain they would ever see, and thanked me for it, as if it was me who had given them the sky and the clouds.

"Ma cherie, let's work on *le futur proche*, or if you prefer we can choose another tense," one of them, Monsieur Duchemin, would beseech me every afternoon. He told me that a man had died on every step of the narrow staircase of La Maison Communale, from the first floor to the last. "Monsieur Fishgrund, for example, may meet his maker soon, ma cherie," Duchemin told me one day. "Albert should make him pay his rent in advance. One never knows with us, we old fellows."

I lived in Maison Communale too, but I didn't actually pay Albert rent. He "visited" me one or more nights a week, always *très gentil*, very kind. On those evenings he brought wine, cooked our dinner, and lit candles. Of course it always rained, but if suddenly the clouds sank to the bottom of the sky and the raindrops died on the roofs, Albert would say, "Let's go for a walk in Josaphat, ma cherie."

There were times when I hated the park. You see, I worked for a retired infantry-major, Jacques, who, in his residence at La Maison Communale, wrote novels for five hours every day. In the evenings I edited his prose, feeling his words and his eyes on my skin, his cat, all the time, purring in his lap. The retired major was Albert's best friend.

I hated going for walks with them in Josaphat, so often the two friends jogged side by side in the drizzle, while I stayed back and made salads for the pensioners, listening to them debate whether Monsieur Duchemin would piss in his pants before dinner, and who would later accompany me to my apartment, Albert, or the major—the old guys called the major *Jacques le Fou*, Crazy Jacques.

Often, after jogging was over, Albert and the major would toss a coin to decide just who was to "walk me home" that night, a term I considered absurd, since the three of us lived in the same building. The tenants in this La Maison Communale, the pensioners, went to bed at 8 p.m., dreaming about rain. From time to time Crazy Jacques appeared on TV and spoke cleverly and at length on his books and his understanding of the world. On nights when he won the toss, he cooked, say, *filet mignon brusselois* with white wine for me, but very often in the middle of the *filet mignon brusselois* he would blurt out, "We should hurry up," which meant that the evening would follow the scenario I knew all too well.

If Albert won the toss, he would arrive at 9 p.m. sharp, whereas Crazy Jacques was often "ready" even before 8:30. Jacques's love was like a dry and voluminous TV show, like the ones in which he took part. He never told me I was pretty, never said I was pleasant company, and I wondered why he kept on tossing the coin in that cold park for the late-evening time with me.

Probably Crazy Jacques really only showed up in my apartment in order to describe the episode later in one of his experimental novels—he had already written three of them in which I was the protagonist, a woman who arrived in the clean, generous city of Brussels from Eastern Europe to look for truth and to learn to speak French. In all three novels I, though not quite cleverly, was Monsieur Jacques's beloved, whom he took from under his best friend's—that would be, but with a fictional name, Albert's—nose. Jacques' novels were highly praised if unreadable, and it constantly rained in them; not a single page with sunny weather.

Crazy Jacques liked to ask me why didn't I marry Monsieur Duchemin. "The old grouch admires your salads, ma cherie. All in Maison Communale know that. He'll die soon, and you'd inherit his collection of Belgian banknotes, which is quite substantial. He has a good car and, as far as I know, he owns a magnifique villa in the town of Ghent, which he rents out."

"I can't marry him because either you or Albert—after tossing a coin—will show up five minutes into the honeymoon," I said.

***

Chez Albert was the strangest pub in the neighborhood. Albert sold only fruit beer. There was cherry beer, which the pensioners nicknamed "Sweet July death," mountain berry beer, and a special brand of diet carrot beer. Albert came by to give me a test in French immediately after his best friend, the retired Major le Fou, took his dry love back to his splendid, always parked,car, the one he bought at an advantageous price from a dying pensioner. After love was over, Monsieur Jacques le Fou often left his old electrical appliances for me as tokens of his appreciation.

"I almost never touched them, ma cherie." Jacques said. "An iron, but what an iron! It's produced by the renowned French company Braun! There is a washing machine for you! And that bicycle is a Shimano!" Two vacant apartments in our building were stuffed with objects Crazy Jacques had given me as presents. He liked it when his love blazed a tangible trail in its wake. "Is Albert better than me?" Jacques asked me. "Did he recite to you some of his new poems?"

Yes, he is "better" than you, I silently admitted to myself.

Albert wrote his poems in a way that made me think of the pensioners' very last rain, and of the sweetish fruit beer they drank in Chez Albert. Albert recently penned that on July 15th it would stop raining, because in July he loved me the way the sky loved its clouds, quietly and sadly. "Tomorrow the rain will be for you, ma cherie," he wrote. Albert's love was peaceful, like beer made of forest berries, timid and aromatic, doing no harm, its sparkling depths as infinite as my dreams about Bulgarian summers. His love made me imagine I sat in a village pub with an old drunkard who had a row of empty glasses on the table in front of him. Though I just knew it rained outside that pub, too, and its parking lot was perpetually empty.

Albert never asked me about Crazy Jacques' new novel, and never said his best friend the major was crazy. He called him, "My poor old friend. My poor old friend Jacques wrote again in a novel that he stole you from me."

***

In summer, tired of their battle against the rain, Brussels would call it a day and go to sleep under the roof of some deserted bus stop; Albert would close the pub until the evening. Then the three of us, Crazy Jacques, radiant after his umpteenth TV appearance, Albert and I would go out together to get drunk on vodka. We drank in the garden behind Crazy Jacques's so-called 'holiday villa.' I sat between them, feeling their arms about my shoulders. We drank and hugged, we held each other, our shoulders pressing tightly; we took slow quiet walks along Avenue des Mimosas. I strode in the middle, one man to either side of me, and it rained all over the place. Jacques had bought an enormous piece of oilcloth. We hid under it, wrapping it tightly around us and ambled on until Avenue des Mimosas melted under the wet raincoat of the sky. We felt the wind in our bones, and at Meiser Square the two men again prepared to toss a coin for me.

I wondered who was to see me off to sleep that night. Would love be a pine forest and a country pub, or would it be a glamorous and silly TV show? Sometimes I didn't want them to toss that coin. I took it from them and threw it into the fountain, then we'd stand under the streetlamp until one of them came up with another coin.

"What if you and I ran away to the Netherlands," Jacques said, "and left Albert in the lurch? What do you say to that?" Yes, Jacques le Fou asked me this one day, but I already knew such could never happen. Albert was his best friend. Yet there were reasons I was Jacques le Fou's best friend, too.

But I knew I couldn't go on living like that. Anyway, I was sure all would end on July 15th when, Albert promised me, there would be sun in the sky. But, didn't the oilcloth feel wonderfully cozy when the three of us huddled together under it, the rainy evenings beautiful like kisses all along the way to Pierard Avenue? Walking, hugging, I between the two men, and Meiser Square heavy with the moon, it folding around our shoulders.

"You are very pretty," Albert said to me, but Jacques snorted, "Don't believe his lies."

Then Albert said, "Stay with me if it doesn't rain on July 15th, I marry you, and Jacques can marry his French publisher. Let us leave the rain to toss the coin for us!"

***

Every evening, as I watched the quiet Arab women, wrapped in their brown silence and black clothes, taking walks in Josaphat Park, flocks of children babbling in their wake, I wished I were a raven trying to perch on their hands.

When the 15th of July came it rained so badly that the streets turned to streams. Monsieur Duchemin was still alive and phoned asking me to become his wife.

Albert and Jacques waited in Chez Albert, and although the 15th was a Saturday night, Albert had closed the pub early and they were drinking vodka inside when I arrived.

"It's raining," Crazy Jacques said, smiling.

It was a long way to Meiser Square where we went every time to toss the coin.

"What will you do with Monsieur Duchemin?" Albert asked me, very seriously, but even a glancing contemplation of what my answer might be made me shy away from all thoughts of the past and the future.

Then the three of us—I, as always, between them, Jacques on my right, Albert to the side of the privet hedge—trudged through the clouds and rain to Meiser Square. Our clothes became sodden within seconds.

"There's no use tossing a coin," Albert said suddenly. "Because it feels to me as if the sun is shining. In fact, it's the brightest sun Brussels has had for two centuries now!" The rain continued to pour down.

First I thought of that distant-village pub and Albert, but then suddenly I thought more deeply of Crazy Jacques. I was his novels' eternal protagonist, after all, so I, not Albert, was actually his best friend.

There was a 50% chance, "We'd better toss a coin," I said.

LYUDA

The vineyards withered in the heat, yellowish-green like the clouds in the sky. The clouds were wild hammers that killed the sun but gave no fresh air. Lyuda didn't care about the sky. The vineyards stretched endless before her, she rode her old horse Matey through the hot leaves, cursing under her breath. Not a living soul was in sight, only the yellow road, full of sun, climbed the hill and sank behind its scorched crest. There were only old men in that village. They wore their new suits and dreamt of naphthalene, killing moths in the air around them. Her husband went to Italy, to Julia Nova or another damn place at the back of beyond, and left her with the old funeral suits of the geezers and their drooling son who howled no matter if it hailed, rained or the clouds just beat it towards the town of Radomir, leaving the sky ugly and hot above her house. Lyuda lived with her mother-in-law, at the end of the village. She could not stand it any longer in that heat, with her wailing baby and the constant chatter of her mother-in-law, a woman who left bread for the ravens.

There was a guy, Stoycho by name, in the neighboring village. He was single. She made up her mind to take her son to doc Petrov and drop in at Stoycho's place on her way back. There was nothing wrong with her son, nothing really, but she wanted to see that Stoycho guy. She was young and the clouds bothered her. She rode their toothless horse Matey through the scorching vineyards, through the dusty maize fields, then through the pepper garden she had to water in the afternoon, all the time thinking, why are there only old men in that lousy village. They were so many, the old geezers, more than the stones on the road. In the neighboring village, Stoycho lived with his mother. Rumors had it his heart was weak and gave him trouble.

Well, her baby son howled as though there was fire burning in his mouth when Lyuda entered Stoycho's house. Stoycho's mother, the old darling, started treating Lyuda to blackberry jam. I made it for Stoycho, you know, she explained. The old hen could have taken the baby for a while, Lyuda thought then said, "Aunt Dimka, can you mind my little

Pavel while I go to the next room. I'd like to ask your son about a problem I have with my raspberries."

Then she turned to Stoycho, "Stoycho, let me see that magazine you have about the worms that eat the roots of raspberries." When the two of them went to his room and he, scraggly and yellow in the face like the withered maize, bent over a basket full of old issues of Bulgarian Agriculture Magazine, she said, "Stop that," and pressed against him. He was thin and gaunt, like her mother-in-law's dog. Her mother-in-law was as stingy as a vice and she thought the mutt could well live on the rats he chased. Stoycho bent under Lyuda's weight, cold like a bottle of lemonade in a fridge, though it was baking hot in the room. The horizon moaned, warped by the burden of the noon. The sky had a swollen cheek and the bad tooth in it was the sun. "Don't talk," she said, paying no attention his face went scarlet like a packet of red pepper. He gasped and he choked but she swallowed his hiccups and her blouse took the cold lemonade of his body. "Pavel is crying, Lyuda!" Stoycho's mother shouted from the other side of the door.

"Crying won't do him any harm," Lyuda said, pressing hard against Stoycho's weak heart.

"Lyuda, come! That child of yours will burst! He's wailing!" the other side of the door shouted. Pavel, like a volcano, spurted out another howl.

"Did you find the magazine, Stoycho?" his mother shrieked .

"Not yet." His words sank into Lyuda's mouth.

"Come tomorrow at my place, the house under the willows. You know where it is," Lyuda whispered, then jumped, opened the door and took her son from the arms of the old woman. The baby's shirt was wet down to his belly button.

"Doc Petrov said he's got a third tonsil in his throat. He'll spit and spatter like that util we cut it. But Pavel is still a baby, the doc said, and we'll have to wait a year or two," Lyuda explained, suckling her son. She had plenty of milk, " I'm like a cow," she said unhappily. Her breasts weighed like sacks, she had filled Stoycho's mouth and eyes with her milk, too. She had soiled his shirt, and it was a pity there was not another baby nearby she could suckle. It fact there was one, a six month old girl in a village further down by the river. Her milk was clean and strong like a cement road, so why should she waste it? Pavel put on a kilo every month with her milk, and every old man and every old woman who had trouble with their sight asked Lyuda to sprinkle some of her strong milk in the bad eye, and the eye healed.

Her mother-in-law cured some rash on her stomach with Lyuda's milk, too. When the old men cut their hands while they chopped the grass for the small chickens, they brought their cut fingers, Lyuda squirted her milk on the cut and they watched her breasts, round like the clouds above the hill. But what could old men do? Her husband picked rotten olives somewhere in Italy, and she tortured poor Stoycho. The guy was thinner than his own shirt. Didn't that vineyard have an end? Her horse, Matey, was exhausted; he could hardly drag his own hooves forward, and Pavel, swimming in his own drool, had finally fallen asleep.

Her breasts were swollen and hurt her, she had to squeeze the milk out of them, and she hated to do that. Pavel was a lazy baby with wrong tonsils in his mouth, and he made no big efforts to suck her milk. Her breasts squirted white rivulets on his cheeks and wetted him even more. She had heard women's milk was expensive in the town of Pernik, but the ticket for the bus was so expensive she forgot about that right away. If only she could get rid of that milk. Far away, by the road that sank into the clouds and the pieces of tattered sky, she noticed several brown dots as big as fleas. Yes, that was Boko's herd of sheep. Oh My, how come she had forgotten about Boko. He was the second single man in the district and lived in a whitewashed house in the village of Opal. He drove his sheep as if they were infantrymen from one mountain to another, all the while swearing his throat off. He was shorter than the ram whose horns he decorated with geraniums.

Boko had a tractor as well, and last year, when Lyuda's husband still hadn't started itching to bury himself in Italy, Boko got drunk like an eel and drove his tractor through her mother-in-law's barn. It was then that Lyuda figured out Boko was as tall as her chin, but now when her breasts weighed a sheep each with that milk in them, she didn't think about her chin.

Lyuda had to go and water the pepper garden. In the evening, she had to weed it. That dammed pepper! The more she hated it the stronger it grew. Every stalk was covered with big white blooms. The weeds in the pepper garden could hardly wait for her to turn around and suckle Pavel. They quickly threw their seeds behind her back, and on the following day they had already sprouted big and leafy. Does Boko pass by the canal or by the river on his way home with his herd, Lyuda wondered. The village of Opal was in the midst of the wilderness. The old men there were more than the flies, the old women did not like her at all. There was not even a doctor there so she could not take Pavel to have his tonsils checked again. Boko lived with his mother if the old nanny-goat still had not met her maker in that heat. Imagine the two hours' ride Matey would have to limp before he hauled his old hooves to Opal. Finally, Lyuda came up with an answer. Boko mowed the old men's meadows and took a 2 liter bottle of brandy an acre. She'd ask him to come and mow their Pop's meadow under the vineyard. Bullshit, Lyuda said to herself. I can mow that meadow myself. A toddler could. Why should I ask Boko when he's as tall as my tits? If you're so smart, tell me how you'll bring him here then. He'll get drunk and he'll fall asleep in the middle of the road. So what, Lyuda reasoned. She'll go and find him.

At that moment Pavel wailed again. She had forgotten the bottle with his water in the box with Stoycho's magazines. Everybody who could run or drive moved to live in Pernik, but her husband, she wished he'd choked on a rotten olive in Italy, left her in the old village so she wouldn't think of bad things. There were two younger men in the three villages; the first on his deathbed, his heart weak like a bottle of the local beer. The second could not walk half a mile without falling drunk after the first hundred steps he took.

Oh, her smart husband that tiptoed to pick olives in Italy! He had calculated it all. She'd water the pepper garden all the time. Her father-in-law, too, was in Italy, picking olives, although it was high time he put on his new naphthalene suit and prepared for the better world where all water was brandy, and there were two pubs on each cloud. Lyuda wished there was another baby she could suckle. Her breasts hurt in the heat. How come that milk in them doesn't go sour, she wondered. Lyuda's husband left her the old Moskvich car all busted up. She could not start it and couldn't drive to Pernik. If you took a peep in a pub there, no matter which pub, you'd see a man who was tall to the ceiling and his heart never gave him the slightest trouble. "Don't go, Plamen. Don't go to

106

pluck those frigging olives in Italy. You know what we do in the morning and in the evening. Forget about money. We'll sell the wine. We'll sell the Moskvich, too. Pavel doesn't eat much. He's okay with my milk, and I am full of it like a dairy. I have the feeling that if you touched me below, milk will run from there, too. Before he went to climb the olives trees like a gorilla, her husband didn't go out of bed for four days.

"Are you ill, son?" her mother-in-law asked, concerned.

Lyuda was very angry, indeed. "He's not ill at all, woman. He is with me. He protects my milk from getting sour. What will Pavel eat if that happened?"

Before Plamen, her husband, left for Italy, he told her, "Don't look at anybody. Listen to me carefully. Don't look at anybody. If you do, I'll kill you when I come back. You know I can always detect when you've looked at another man."

Who can I look at, Plamen? You don't have breasts that weigh a 5 gallon barrel each, and there is no other baby but Pavel to suckle, the vineyard has no end, sugar beet field has no end. You pluck these fucking olives in Italy and I'll stay here. Squirt more milk into the old men's eyes? In all the three villages, there is no old man whose eyes I had not squeezed milk into at least twice. Come on, Matey, old horse. We are still not going home, you know. I have to weed the pepper garden.

Lyuda bent down to weed the pepper. She left Pavel on his white sheet and she weeded, and weeded, and weeded until the pile of sour weeds became taller than Boko. It was good that Pavel started screaming, for she suckled him and relieved her breasts. Suddenly she remembered there was another baby in the village of Vladimir, the six month old girl. Petrana and Petar had adopted her. They couldn't have children for twelve years and when the small thing squeaked in their house things became happy and peaceful. Petrana and Petar went to live in Pernik first, but there was more smoke than air there and the baby was a puny one. It didn't put enough weight, so in the beginning Lyuda wondered if its heart was Okay. When the little Yana fed a month on her milk, the little thing buckled up.

Come on, Matey, old boy, let's go to Petrana and Petko's place to give weak Yana some milk. I hope she'll drink much this evening and make my breast easy. And you, lazy, lazy guy, she turned to her son

Pavel. You couldn't suck all my milk. Well, it's not your fault that I am like a cow. Lyuda rode five miles of the road that was full of sunset and warm wind, before she made it to Petrana and Petar's place. She saw Petar, big and slow, milking the cow in the barn, but didn't say anything to him.

"Petrana," Lyuda called out. "Bring little Yana here. I'll suckle her. You prepare a clean bottle and I'll fill it with milk for her. Quick, woman, quick. I'll burst like a grenade with that milk. Petrana, wash my Pavel, please, while I give suck to your Yana. Then give me something to eat. I'm starving. I ate only raspberries today. My belly's full of raspberries, my milk is raspberries and a million raspberry thorns are in my fingers. I'm afraid I may scratch your Yana. Yana, treasure, smile at me. Smile." Petrana, who had been waiting twelve years for a baby, gave Pavel his bath smiling happily. She touched him so lovingly as if the boy didn't have his drool all over him. Lyda noticed Petar's eyes on her breast as she suckled small Yana. Petar is okay, Lyuda thought then she turned around and saw Petrana ladle out delicious soup in the plates on the table. "I'll give you more soup, Lyuda," she said beaming with happiness. "You give the kids your strong milk.

"Yes, it's strong," Lyuda said. For a split second she looked at Petar. A drop of milk dripped from her on Yana's neck. She was a lazy baby, too, and Lyuda had to pinch her nose to wake her up. Yes. It was true Petar's hair was gray. It was true he wore old patched trousers that smelled of dogs and manure, but Lyuda smelled of Matey, of dust and of horse's saddle. So what. Let her husband pluck olives. It served him right. Don't go to Italy, Plamen, please. Please, don't go. I cannot live without you. Plamen held her fifteen minutes in his arms before he caught the bus to Italy. He and his father almost missed it on account of that.

It was true Petar's back was hunched, but, on the other hand, if it wasn't that hunched, he'd pack and go to Radomir to make twice as much money. Here he planted potatoes, herded cows and mowed for the old women. He was with his wife and probably every morning he held her in his arms.

Lyuda ate three plates of the soup, then Petrana went to bring some cherries. She had plucked them today, she said, so Lyuda could have some cherry vitamins in her milk for the kids.

While Petrana went out for the cherries, Lyuda looked at Petar once again, then started squeezing milk into the bottle for little Yana. Then she looked at hunchbacked Petar. He shook in his soiled pants, patched at the knees. She saw his face. Although it was tanned by the sun, it changed color, now red, now black around his eyes. The two babies slept quietly on the couch, Pavel's tonsils slept as well. Petrana had dressed Pavel in a pair of her daughter's pants.

Petrana came back with the cherries, a big, full bag of them, and Petar said, "I'll go and give Matey some barley. Poor soul, he's been under the scorching sun all day."

"I was there, too," Lyuda told him. She thought she was stronger than Matey, but didn't say so. The two women talked about Pavel's tonsils, and about fruit juices they were supposed to give the babies. Finally, she wrapped Pavel in his white sheet, propped him with a pillow on the couch and went to check Matey that was blissfully chewing his barley. Petar smoked by his side, the cigarette like an open wound on his mouth.

He stood up and moved restlessly as Lyuda approached him, then left his place to make way for her, but she did not go the way he had made for her. She went directly against him, she collided with him, with his old patched trousers, and with his shirt she collided, making it all wet with her milk. Stay quiet, she said. Yes, it was true he smelled exactly as Matey did, like the stables at the end of the village. But if one took a walk through the vineyard or if one weeded the pepper garden, one stopped smelling of Matey. "Wait. Wait," she said. He was hot like the stones of the stream that had run dry under the heat of the yellow clouds. She thought she had squeezed all her milk into that bottle, but Petar's chest was white all over with it. Then his shirt was a white cemented shield and her milk was stronger than ever.

"Now go to Petrana. Quick. Hold them in your arms, both of them, Petrana and Yana," she whispered into his ear. But then, again, Lyuda didn't go the way he had made for her. She bumped into his soiled pants, patched at the knees, for a second time. Pavel suddenly wept and kicked in little Yana's pants that he had already wetted. Matey went on eating his barley, the best food the old horse had seen for years.

"You are so late. Where did you go?" her mother-in-law asked when Lyuda came home and left Pavel on the bed, wet like a fish, drool and milk all over him. His tonsils were evidently at work again, ruining the little guy's peace and quiet.

"I visited aunt Petrana and uncle Petar, " Lyuda answered. "I suckled little Yana. She is as thin as wire. I left her a bottle of milk, too, and while Matey chewed his barley, Petrana gave me something delicious to eat." "Good. It's good you help her with that child," her mother-in-law said. "Petrana's had hard times, those doctors, hospitals and all. But now that she has her Yana, she's settled down. Listen, your aunt Malina came and said that the grass in our Pop's meadow was ripe enough. You have to mow it, Lyuda. Tomorrow, or the day after tomorrow. Listen, I almost forgot. Stoycho came here an hour ago. He brought some agricultural magazine for you. There's something in it about worms in the raspberries. I thought there were no worms on the raspberries this year. He left ten minutes ago ... long and thin like a thread. His heart's no good. I am sorry for him."

"I am sorry for him, too," Lyuda heaved a sigh.

"The poor soul," the old woman went on. "He plodded five kilometers in the heat to tell you about that worm. He trudged all that dusty road in vain. I am sorry for him, he is a sick man."

"I wish I came back half an hour earlier," Lyuda said.

Pavel turned around on the bed and gave out a howl. It sounded like he had a beehive in his mouth. Lyuda gave him her breast. She had suckled little Yana, she had left a liquorice bottle, full of milk for her and she dripped milk again. Where did that milk come from? She was afraid to think what would happen when the grapes would be ripe. Then probably she'd drip a white milky path after Matey's tail in the fields. She wished she could go to Pernik. Women's milk there was more expensive than these bottles of French perfume, which transformed you into a lady. Never in her life had such a lady weeded a pepper garden, nor shoveled manure into a truck. There was not even one old man in Pernik, and not one old-fashioned suit. The pubs there were full of tall men. Well, her husband Plamen held her fifteen minutes in his arms before he caught that bus, it was true. But how could she live with fifteen minutes a whole year until Plamen made enough money to buy an apartment in Pernik?

Plamen, don't go. I can't live without you, she said several times, but he went.

Now she wished she had come back home earlier. Stoycho could have told her about the worm that ate the roots of the raspberries

"Lyuda," her mother-in-law said, "you send a word to Boko...Oh, don't tell me you don't remember who Boko is. A small guy, as short as a keg. He's a shepherd."

"Yes, yes. I know him," Lyuda said and wiped the milk from her son's cheek.

"You told my cousin to go and ask Boko to come and mow our Pop's meadow. Didn't you mow that meadow last year, Yuda? You did, and you were pregnant at that time. Yes, I remember. You had Pavel in your big belly when you mowed it."

"We'll see, "Lyuda said. "I have to dig the vineyard, I have to put manure in the bean field and I have to water the maize. I have to pick the raspberries, too, so I said to myself that Boko could help us."

"Well, yes. You know these things better than I do. I forgot to tell you that Boko, the poor guy is no bigger than one of his sheep, you know. And he didn't grow up because he drank from an early age. So Boko came here in the afternoon to ask when you wanted him to mow our Pop's meadow. Lyuda, give me a glass of water, will you?"

Lyuda gave her some water and the old woman went on, "Boko said that tomorrow he'd find you in the maize field under the vineyard. You'll go to water the maize tomorrow, won't you? Tell the guy when he's to start mowing. Oh, you are blessed with your milk, you can take my word for that. And Pavel is such a handsome baby, Lyuda. Let me touch wood. Let me touch wood just in case. He sucks your milk as vigorously as a calf, and he's so strong. Lyuda, tomorrow, about seven p.m. in the maize field. Boko will come there and talk to you about Pop's meadow. Did you hear me. Lyda?"

She had told Plamen not to go to Italy. We'll make enough money, she had said. But he was hard-headed, he went to pick the rotten olives there.

"Yes, I heard you, "Lyda muttered. "I'll be waiting for him there in the maize field, under our Pop's meadow."

IMPOSSIBLY BLUE

Sometimes the sea was quiet and the sun was in the sky all the time, or so I thought. I was tempted to run to the shore and get a swim, but I suspected a storm would break the minute I'd touch the water. That was my imagination, of course. I could hear the wind roar and howl and the waves hurled masses of cold rage against the other side of the page. I wrote a short story on the page, but on its other side the ocean growled. The paper was the wall that separated me from the endless freezing water. At times, I asked myself what would happen if I bored a hole in the page, I had even bought a penknife which I kept on my desk. I often forgot what I was writing as I sat there lost, motionless, listening.

"What are you doing?" Len, my husband, asked and I thought I saw fright in his eyes. I didn't tell him about the crags, the surf, the waves hitting against the rocks. I didn't tell him I heard screams of dying birds but he sensed something had gone wrong with me.

"You are unhappy your stories don't sell," he muttered. "Don't be. Stories are nothing. Come here."

When I was with him I couldn't hear the ocean. I was afraid I would miss the rare sunny hours when the waves slept and barely touched the paper on the other side. Those were the prettiest days in my life. I glued my ear to the paper and listened. At first it was only the sigh of rippling water, then sands whispered and the shore was so near I could feel its pebbles on the tips of my fingers.

"You don't speak to our son," Len said. "He needs you. You don't smile at him. You don't notice me."

We had a small house on the shore of the Black Sea. It was Len who bought it. I had never liked the sea. It raged and thundered in winter, in summer tourists infested the shore and the beach was full of them. I turned my back to the waves. Sometimes I swam at night when the beach was a sigh in the air. Then the surf and the night blended and the shore touched the page with the ocean I had left on my desk.

"Maybe I am in love with another woman," my husband said.

What a funny man he is, I thought. You are free to be in love with anyone you want. You are free but I am not, Len. I want to go behind the page.

"Mother, why don't you write on your computer?" my son asked. "You write nothing on that piece of paper. You are constantly staring at it at. There's nothing behind it, Mother."

But I heard slight barely audible tapping on the other side of the page. At first I thought it was a pebble that had hit the paper. Then fear seized me. I thought the sharp edges would cut a hole and my page would be torn into pieces. I panicked. What if the water burst into the house? My son was in his room. My son!

"Do you want me to take you to the other side?" I asked the boy. "There are sunny days there, and the waves are quiet like the pictures on the walls in your room. The water is warm."

"I like the Black Sea more than your page," my son said. "Your page is a lie. You care about an empty piece of paper."

The tapping sound on my page got stronger. I could swear somebody was typing on the other side. The surf was writing a short story for its shore.

The noise stopped abruptly and then the sunniest day behind the page began. I could swear there were seagulls flitting over the surface of the water, the sun shone, and infinity loved me. I reached for the penknife that lay on my desk. I wanted to get there, behind the page.

"I have to go," Len, my husband, said.

"Go," I told him. "You are a free man".

"You used to be so jealous," he breathed. "What's wrong with you?"

"It's what she sees behind the paper," my son said. "The page's changed her."

They'd been gone for a month, my son and my husband, or so I thought. I had not written any stories. I described the sounds the water was making. They were magnificent and powerful. The page was the only barrier that cut me off from my dreams. Maybe Len and my son were at home all the time. Yes, somebody cooked food for me, and I didn't care what had happened to the woman Len was in love with. The tapping sounds on the other side of the paper continued. The ocean was friendly and I thought of the writer on the other side of the page. He was not as tall and handsome as my husband. I believed his face was brown with the sun, and he was tired because he had been writing on the water months on end, and there was no one to read his fairytales. I felt sorry for him and I tapped the page with a sharp pencil. He answered me. He tapped the paper so carefully, so timidly I could have cried.

"There is no ocean behind the paper and there is no one typing there," my husband, who was in love with another woman, said. "I want you to be happy the way you were before you found the notebook with a single page in it."

He didn't know these were the loveliest hours redolent of salty water, soothing with the shrieks of seagulls. Was the ocean a string of days I had missed, days that had gone leaving no memory, no trace? Who had settled on the other side of the paper? I lived with my stories in the smallest room, in the unreality of water, on the shore of an angry black sea. I had a husband who was in love with another woman and a son who needed my attention all the time.

They were not a part of my happy days. Maybe the shore on the other side of the page was the place where death waited for me, tapping ever so gently on the thin white sheet, letting me know it was much more real than my uneventful life, and the short story I'd printed on the paper was a door to oceans I had never seen. Was it my hope to go there that made a difference? The man, the one who was not very tall and handsome, lived in the story.

He had a long purple scar on his cheek. I like your blue T-shirt, he had said to me. I'll come and find you no matter what. And I'll bring you a blue tulip. There are no blue tulips, the woman who lived in my short story had said. I was that woman. I lived in the words and the paper pulled me out of the stormy waters. I'll bring you a blue tulip, the man repeated and the story ended abruptly. Maybe the biting winds behind the page were my panic, I'd never see the tulip. My hopes surged, gleamed, then were gone, and I knew they would not come back. My husband's shadow was my home, my room was made of fears, and the waves behind the page hated the night.

"I've torn the page from your notebook," my husband said. "I burned it."

I froze in my tracks. I had no notebook and no ocean. No soothing smell of salt and infinity. I looked at my desk, horrified.

"Our son needs you. I need you," my husband said. "I want you to be healthy. There was nothing behind that page. Nothing."

In the evening, I cooked potato soup for them. In the morning, I took my son to the zoo. I hadn't taken him anywhere for months. We ate ice-cream and sandwiches, he told me tales. I listened, I listened hard. The waves were gone. There was no ocean and no seagulls. My son babbled on. My husband brought me flowers and suggested the three of us go to France, to the castles on the Loire, and the French Riviera. I wanted to stay home. I bought a new notebook, and then another one. None of their pages separated me from an ocean of fears and hopes, from squalls and tales of screaming waves. I locked myself in the room and listened. I glued blank pages on the wall and nothing happened. Death and fears had left me, hopes had left me, too.

My husband brought me flowers almost every day; my son was happy and cheerful. We invited friends and threw parties. You are beautiful, Anna. You are more beautiful than before. I am so happy you are back, my husband said. He didn't know I kept a sheet of crumpled paper glued to my skin. I prayed to bring the ocean back to me. But the salty wind was gone.

I took a job in the local library. I cooked delicious meals for my family, I took long walks with friends, and I wrote short stories and fairy tales.

"We can go to see the castles on the Loire, what do you think?" My husband said.

I thought I wanted to go.

"I'm glad the yellow rings under your eyes are gone. I am glad you smile again."

Rarely, at night I heard the waves beat against sharp stones. I heard screams of seagulls, I saw the page again and I wrote on it. The endless water glowed, I wanted to swim to the shore, and I sensed the wind slept in the waves. Very rarely, I heard the tapping sounds and deep in my memories the short story gleamed, pale and silvery, like a shadow of a kite, like a song I had forgotten long ago but it was in the air I breathed.

I was a happy woman again. I had my job and my family. The ocean had vanished and the wind had died. I was free.

On the day before we started for the ancient castles on the Loire, my son and my husband went to buy a new suitcase. I was in the kitchen cooking lunch when the front door bell rang.

"Coming," I called out, thinking it was my husband with the new suitcase.

Out of breath, I ran to see it.

A man, not very tall, not very handsome, stood in the door. A long scarlet scar ran down his cheek. I looked at it. I looked at it and could not breathe.

"This is for you," the man said.

He gave me a flower, a tulip.

It was blue.

Impossibly blue.

DONO

The men from Dono's clan, broad-shouldered and surly, squashed the words between their teeth and the mere hissing sound left others guessing what had to be obeyed. But they all obeyed Dono. His wish was law. Everyone was shattered under it. At the age of twenty five, he became the chieftain of the carters of the whole district and made it clear that he would not endure dissension or disturbance. Dono gathered all his men and, watched by hundreds of eyes, broke the former chieftain's right hand. The thieves who terrorized the caravans of carts in the Slavic gorge near Sofia were scared out of their wits; a day later Dono set fire to their homes.

One of the thieves, thin and tall like a lamp post nicknamed Hunchback, became Dono's groom. The man's back was crooked, his shoulders were bony and drooping. Hunchback was Dono's servant and had sufficient nerve to stare at his patron's face, flooding it with hatred of his black, glowing eyes. Dono found perverse pleasure in egging on Hunchback's venom. It bespoke weakness, so apparent and tangible, that it had driven Hunchback's eyes deep into his skull; a thick and lasting impotence that the chieftain could play with.

Woe to Hunchback if Lisso, Dono's horse, did not jump when the patron caught sun beams in a mirror and sent them to the shining back of the stallion. Woe to the servant if a single hair of the horse's tail was entangled with another. Dono knew that his servant's name was Boris, but never called him by it. "Hunchback!" he shouted. And, while the long scraggly man shuffled his bones to answer the call, the chieftain beat the heel of his shoe with a thin willow branch. Black would turn the day for Hunchback if the branch hit the heel of the shoe more than three times.

For the past two months Boris had taken care of Vecka, the chieftain's wife. She couldn't stand on her feet. All women from Dono's clan became ugly a year or two after their weddings. They turned into speechless brooms; canvas sacks from which the young carters elbowed their way into the world. Dono had chosen motherless Vecka, on purpose, so that no one would ask after her. For who, Dono thought, would care anything about one snotty brat among eleven others? Her father? Not likely. The old pouch would kiss his feet if the chieftain threw him a coin. Dono did not need a wife's love; he had squandered passion and jealousy on numerous beauties in Sofia and got tired of it. He did not need a wife for his bed, a carters' chieftain could have the best girl in the district. Yet Dono wanted a wife for his house—to make the windows shine and remove every speck of dust from the floor. He wanted a son from her. He wanted her hands to sweep his stables and her eyes to smile at his guests. He had no relish for talking with her. His wife had to resemble the thieves from the Slavic gorge at whom he took shots with his gun; eight feet away from them he stood, aiming at the forehead. Then Dono could feel his power, which was enormous and straight, like a road without an end.

He could never feel that way when Vecka was near him. Coming back home every day, her voice rolled over him, "I was sly to tie him, I was strong to hide him." It didn't sound like a song; it did not utter words like a human voice. Not a song, but a tremendous roaring whirlwind threshed through his yard, dashed down the hill tearing away the roofs of his cousins' houses, jarring upon his ears, setting his thoughts on fire. He wriggled like a worm with shame. Shame! She made him ashamed! He, Dono, the boss, before whom all carters knelt dumb and tractable! The chieftain, whose word was stronger than the law. The man who possessed more power than the mayor's was made into a fool and a laughingstock. His father had bequeathed all the land of the family to Dono, though he was the youngest of the five brothers. Vecka, his wife; at the very sound of her name he seethed with anger. Year in year out, she gave birth to girls and filled his house with female rubbish. Whenever he approached his home he could hear her shouting that goddamn song.

Rarely, Dono got so enraged that he beat her with his belt. At such moments he tried to imagine her shrieks flooding the quiet houses of his native hamlet and all his cousins would be convinced that he wore the trousers, not Vecka. She thrust her apron in her mouth to stifle the sounds of pain, so he tore up the apron. She then bit the hems of her skirt; he tore up the skirt as well. She learned to bite her fists. Dono could not make her scream. It was the swishing of the belt and Hunchback's bent figure by the door that gave the sign to the villagers that Dono was teaching his wife to respect silence. And always when the swishing ceased, broken and smashed, as slowly as an ant, a song clambered through the window: "I was sly to tie him; I was strong to hide him ...." Then Hunchback's shallow eyes burned.

Dono didn't strike his wife beyond a certain point, for he did not wish to waste his youth in jail. When he went out, the noise of his steps still echoing in the lane, his four daughters quietly crooned, "I was sly to tie him ...," their voices twisted into a rope that knotted the whole house. At such times Dono did not feel like lingering at home. He caught sun beams in a mirror and sent them to the back of the horse then master and stallion vanished down the road to the pub. Hunchback stood motionless at the door.

Once, as Vecka's stifled sobs made the house split with pain, the servant approached her and offered her some wet rags. He was ashamed to watch how the woman put them on her bruised shoulders. He had seen only her naked arm. It did not look like an arm of a woman, its skin resembled a dry stick with a peeled bark. Yet his shallow eyes saw it otherwise. They swept away the scars and Vecka's hand appeared tender and white; the fingers that gave him lunch every day swam before Hunchback enveloping him with fragrance and peace. Every single patch of land where the woman had stepped seemed to whisper her name.

Dono's mother was never young. When his father got on for fifty he imagined he was no good as a carter anymore and sold his horses. But instead of buying a chandler's shop as he had hinted earlier, the old goat took a young girl and disappeared. It was rumored that the couple escaped to Greece and when Dono's father came back dragging the girl after him and looking boldly at people who lowered their eyes, Dono thought he would kill him. His mother died shortly after that and Dono could not learn the end of the tale she had begun telling him in his childhood, the only tale he had ever heard.

The chieftain detested his memories because every time he let them flood back he compared Vecka to his mother. Well, his mother was never beaten; she was a drooping heap of decay by the fireplace and the only sound that compelled her to stir and move about uneasily was the delicate tap-tap of his father's fingers on the table. "I was sly to hide him, I was strong to hide him...." Was it so? Against his own will Dono sometimes crooned that song. Vecka's voice was stronger than his hatred.

He never listened further for that would mean he was an inferior man. The straw that broke the camel's back was when Vecka cut Lisso`s tail. The horse's tail that no money could buy! That horse was the only living thing Dono had ever prayed for in his life; Lisso was his friend, the only being that could understand him. The stallion knew everything including Dono's disgrace in having no son. His panic that someday his chieftain's hand would not hold firm and a pert youngster would come and break it, as Dono himself had done to the former chieftain. And his vixen wife had stunted his best friend; the horse with a velvety hide and deep brown eyes that spoke to Dono`s soul. "You are not only a master to me. You are my road, my water, my life. No foul money stands between us. No lies." Vecka had cut Lisso's tail! She had destroyed that wild silver whirlwind. No, Dono would never forgive her.

How could his father order around his mother, the old grey woman, forcing her to work and toil until every single saucer and piece of furniture shone? When the house was clean, she would squat in the corner, mute and unnecessary like a pair of old shoes. Dono was richer than his father, ten times richer. So why didn't the carter break the brown porcelain cup from which his wife drank milk in the morning? Why, Lisso?

He'd show her!

The moment before the iron clasp of the belt hit Vecka's grey dress, someone clutched at Dono`s throat.

"I cut the tail!"

Hunchback, the servant, was looking at him with his shallow wild eyes.

"You?" the carter hissed back. "You?"

"I cut it."

"No!" Vecka shouted. "I did it."

"Who cut Lisso`s tail!"

"I!"

"I!"

The voices of his wife and Hunchback roared out together. Dono could hear nothing more. His four daughters were looking through the window like four drab mice. Dono didn't care. He could hear Hunchback's husky voice singing, "I was sly to tie him, I was strong to..."

122

"Stop, please, Boris, stop!" his wife shouted.

What? What did she call him? Boris? That hunchback! That wretch! Boris!

Vecka began singing again. The bitch. The bitch! Her grey dress. Her loathsome dress. Hit it! Trample on it! Don't sing any more, eh? What about you, little Boris? You rag!

When Dono approached the pub he imagined he could hear their voices twisted into a knot, "I was sly to tie him..." The song pressed down on him, his breath rasped on his lips. The carter let his horse go and lay down on the yellow grass in the sun burnt field. The hot noon sky reeled and touched the earth that burned in the late yellow summer.

PRETTIER

There was a black whirlpool in the Struma River which was not far from our house. The place was wild, overgrown with stubborn willows. You'd break your axe before you cut one of those huge trees and you'd end up disappointed in the end. The wood wouldn't burn; you'd say it was made of bones. A couple of guys died there last summer. Since then, everybody called it Bludgeon pool. My father was that kind of a man; there was a lot of the gnarled willow wood and a lot of the Bludgeon pool in him. He could crush you with his words. He was a wealthy man, too, and very hard to please.

One day a guy, Stancho, passed out while he dug the new vines in Dad's vineyard. Dad shouted, "Bloody faker!" then set the dogs on the man. I saw the mutts biting and clawing Stancho, but he didn't shift, just lay there, sprawling like a heap of cabbages in his dirty clothes. Since that day, folks in these parts dubbed Dad, "Nasty", but he didn't give his nickname much thought. He didn't lose weight on account of it, nor did he complain of any lack of sleep. His face grew darker, it was true, and guys made way when they saw him in the street.

I had a rough time of it when I tried to persuade my father to accept one simple thing; I wanted him to hire Rosko to clean our wine barrels.

"That Rosko is pretty bullheaded," Dad said. "You know he's Stancho's son. Why have you chosen him?"

"Because Rosko will do a good job and because you'll pay him very little for it. His family is flat broke. His father's bakery went bust, and his mother cleans our neighbor's stables. As for Rosko's sister ... look at her. She looks more like a broom than a high school student."

"It's not that," Dad grumbled. "Tell me openly why you want that rascal Rosko to clean our wine barrels."

I had two brothers. Both of them were like the clayey land where the vines in our vineyard grew. When it was hot the clay cracked and you could thrust your whole arm into the crevice. My brothers' minds cracked just as easily, and Dad could shove anything into their heads. The two of them listened to him like calves. Dad knew I was not made of that clay.

I was the one who paid Dad's workers their wages and I checked how much each of them had earned. It made no difference if the fellow fawned over me, whispering, "Hey, you look sexy. You've no idea what I'll do to you if you meet me tonight in the park." Or he simply said, "You bitch."

One day, a worker mowed the meadow near our house and complained he was sick. It was too hot, he said. The sun was intolerable and he wanted to know if he could go home earlier.

"Yes, you can go," I said. "But don't come back tomorrow."

The worker said his nose would bleed and it bled.

"Galla, will you pay me for the work I did today before I go?" the man asked.

"Yes, I will. Come and take your money when everybody else does, at 9 p.m."

The man grumbled a string of obscenities under his breath and then put nettle leaves in his nose. It stopped bleeding and he took to mowing again, every now and then stuffing crushed nettles in his nostrils. After that day, the entire village referred to me as Nettles Galla, or Galla the viper. Vipers, as thick as motorcycle tires, bred in our meadows. So what? I wouldn't pay a guy who wouldn't work hard and made his nose bleed instead.

"You are tough like me," my father said. "There's no blood under your skin. There is slate."

I couldn't care less about the slate under my skin, but I reckoned it would be good the other folks knew about it. I liked it when guys made way for me when I rode my bicycle along the road, and I hated looking at men's backs. Let the guys turn their backs to their wives.

"So, Galla, you want Rosko to scrape and caulk our wine barrels?" Dad repeated, looking me in the eye. "No way. Rex and Buck, those were Dad's two dogs, gnawed through Rosko's father's pants when the bloody faker fainted in my vineyard. The next day the idiot came to thrash me with a stake. I was lucky. Buck and Rex saved my neck."

"Rosko kicked our dogs real bad and busted their ribs," my elder brother chimed in. "I paid the vet a fat bundle to cure them."

"Rosko beat me at the disco!" my younger brother barked, frothing at the mouth. "I think he punctured the tire of my new Peugeot, too!" At

126

that point he was on the verge of muttering a curse, but he took himself in hand. Dad hated it when my brothers cussed in his presence. "I'll pay two thugs to kick his ass the way he deserves."

My mother sat silently at the table. When she heard about Rosko, she heaved a deep sigh. She was given to crying and she'd whimper over her cooking stove for no reason at all. Once I asked her, "What's wrong, Mom? What are you sniffing and sobbing for? We've got money, we've got plenty of food, and we hire guys to work for us. Here, take this handkerchief and blow your nose."

"Galla, I'm not sure you are a good woman. I worry about you."

"Don't," I told her. "I'll be always okay. You can take my word for that."

"Galla, I can scrape the wine barrels if you want me to," my younger brother offered. He'd stoop to wiping the village beggar's snot. "Give Rosko the slip," he advised me.

"I have taken a fancy to Rosko," I said.

"No, you haven't" Dad said.

"Yes, I have," I said. "I've already told him to come to our place. I'll pay him fifty levs per barrel."

"What?" Dad thundered. Every time you told him you'd give a guy fifty levs to clean a wine barrel my father's lumbago gave him big trouble. "You are out of your mind," he declared at last. "I wouldn't fork fifty levs to the Mayor if he came here and said he was willing to scrape my wine barrel."

"Look here, Dad," I said. "I'll give Rosko my money, not yours."

"No, you won't," Dad said.

I could hear Mom sigh in her chair.

"What was that sigh of yours for?" I asked her.

"Listen Galla," she started. "Every time you fancy somebody, the poor guy leaves the village and moves to another part of the country."

"I'm none the worse for my loss," I said, and she once more heaved a deep sigh.

About a year ago, I fell for a young man. The worst part about it all was that the guy's mother was my mom's friend. The lad was suddenly crazy about me. He came day and night to my place 'to shoot the breeze', as he put it. After I said I didn't want to see him, he took to drinking hard. His whole family moved to the town of Radomir, and my mother lost her friend.

"We won't pay anybody fifty levs per barrel," Dad declared.

"You won't pay, but I will," I said. "The barrels are big. A barrel of ours can hold the cow, the bucket in which you milk her and the stool on which you sit."

"I strongly disapprove," Dad muttered and thought hard. Finally he said, "Well, I'm going to give you enough rope to hang yourself."

"A woman ready to give a guy fifty bucks to have him clean her wine barrels won't hang herself," I said. "You can count on that".

"Even our dogs will have no respect for a woman who squanders money on men!" Dad growled.

"A woman who gives Rosko fifty bucks per barrel couldn't care less about Rex and Buck," I said. "The mutts still go with their tails between their legs at the sight of her shadow."

You couldn't imagine what happened when I visited Rosko's place.

His father still had the scars that Rex's and Buck's fangs had dug in his arms, and Rosko wore the pants all patched up after my younger brother's thugs kicked his ass. Rosko's family was having bean soup for lunch when I entered their house. They froze the minute they saw me. It looked as though the food turned into sawdust in their mouths. His mother blew her nose; his father fidgeted and coughed. Rosko, however, didn't bother to look up.

"What do you want with us, Galla?" his mother said. "I wouldn't poke my nose in an honest family's affairs if I were you." That woman had the gift of the gab. She rarely kept her mouth shut, I'll grant her that. Dad was right, she was as noisy as a railway station. Well, she could be dead with all her noises for all I cared.

"Good afternoon, Aunt Dobra," I said. "You look good today. But it's not you I'd like to talk to."

"I haven't invited you to our place," Rosko's father remarked, his eyes gleaming viciously. I made up my mind. I'd buy top quality pork for Rex and Buck. The dogs deserved a reward for having bitten that boor.

"Uncle Stancho, you needn't extend an invitation to me," I said. "I'm not that important. You have an honest family, Uncle Stancho. I come to your home hat in hand. In fact, I come to have a word with Rosko."

128

"You are not welcome here," Rosko said as he gorged himself on his bean soup, his eyes intent on his bowl. I loved it when a guy's family glared at me, the tattered linoleum floor the friendliest thing in sight. I simply adored that!

"Rosko, I'd like to put an end to our long-running feud," I said. Every word I uttered felt like a knife I stuck in my own back. I bowed to them all, but that was something I could live with. "I'd like to make you an offer, Rosko."

"You know where you can stick your offer," he said.

"Why should you say that?" I said, sticking in another knife. "It's true I've made mistakes, but I can correct them. The scales fell from my eyes and I realized I was wrong." I tried to stare him down. "My family did the wrong thing to you and I am here to pay for it."

They stared. I hoped the bean soup had scorched their stomachs. Well, I wouldn't forget to buy Rex and Buck the best pork in the neighborhood. I never forgot insults; they remained in my bones the way the blood of the lambs stuck to the chopping-log after Dad killed them.

"What do you want?" Rosko's father asked gruffly.

"I want nothing from you, Uncle Stancho," I began. "Only a young man can do this job; it's slimy and slippery, and the dregs have congealed at the bottom. One could slip and fall. Uncle Stancho, it upsets me to think of you having a broken leg, you know."

"What's slippery and slimy?" asked Dobra, the woman with the gift of the gab, her eyes clawing me. "Why should you speak about congealed dregs? We have nothing to do with the dregs. Or do you want us to clean your toilets?"

"By no means, Aunt Dobra! I clean my toilet myself. I need a professional hand at scraping wine barrels. We put the most precious thing we have in those barrels—our wine," I explained carefully, watching her. "My father lives for that wine, you know. In the evenings, he drinks half a glass and doesn't allow the rest of us to try it. That's why I came to your place: I'd like to ask Rosko to come and scrape our barrels. I'd like him to prepare them for the new wine. He has both the guts and the skilful hands for the job, I think."

"Who, me?" Rosko cried. "Why don't you clean your own barrels, Nettles? Your poison is enough to disinfect all the wine-cellars in the district."

"Rosko, if I could disinfect them, would I crawl to you for help? Would I trudge all the way to your house? You are the best for the job, Rosko. You can scrape the barrels in a way that will make the new wine swoop down over men like a kettle of hawks. You can make it smell like a pool in the river where naked girls swim."

"It's interesting you speak about naked girls," the railway station woman croaked at me. "Why, Galla, perhaps you've come out as a girl-lover?"

"No, I haven't, Aunt Dobra," I said. "Everybody in these parts say my father's wine makes men think of naked girls, especially when the guys have had too much."

"Your wine makes me think of your father's grave," Rosko's mother said, and the railways in her voice clanged. At that moment I imagined Rex and Buck chewing that pork I'd buy for them. Let the woman cackle on about graves until kingdom come.

"Hey, how much will you pay him per barrel?" Rosko's father said, looking at me shrewdly. He tried hard to concentrate on his bean soup and appear lukewarm about my offer. Of course, he failed. His eyes were about to jump into my mouth.

"If she gives us less than twenty levs per barrel, I'll set the dog on her right away," Rosko's mother said. "That's exactly what Galla deserves."

I knew their dog Pirin, the scraggy mongrel. The fur on his neck had fallen off, and the beast stank of ointments. Poor Pirin whined every time he saw my boots. I had kicked him a couple of times and I guess he'd never forget me.

"We needn't talk about Pirin now," I told Dobra. "Your son is the man I can do business with. I wish all of you well."

"Well my foot!" Rosko's father said, and scratched the scars on his arms. "Rosko won't work for you if you pay him less then twenty-two levs per barrel."

"Look here." Rosko turned to me. "Can you see this pair of sandals by the door?"

"Yes, I can," I answered.

"That's good. Now go and bring the sandals to me. I want you to clean them before I finish my soup."

If I hadn't put so much energy in my project so far, I would have kicked his ass. Perhaps I'd even set fire to their barn with their two nanny-goats inside, and Pirin who slept like a log on the straw. I knew better than that. I had to put up with the flames and the poison that spewed from Rosko's mouth. I wanted our wine redolent of skies and summer nights.

I brought Rosko the sandals. They were a sorry sight. Their straps were frayed, trodden. I left the pair in front of Rosko, watching his toes. They were covered with a layer of dust that was at least an inch thick.

"I want thirty levs per barrel," Rosko declared. At that moment, his father choked on his own tongue. His mother was suddenly speechless. After a couple of seconds she banged a heavy fist on the table. I kept silent.

"Thirty levs per barrel and I want you to put the sandals on my feet," Rosko said.

Come on, I thought to myself. You've shoveled cow dung and chicken droppings onto trucks, you've dug heaps of manure and those heaps have been often taller than you, girl.Rosko's dirty feet won't frighten you.

"I'll give you forty levs per barrel, but I won't put the sandals on your feet," I said. I played a trump and hoped to win the game.

Rosko's father poured a spoonful of soup onto the tablecloth instead of putting it in his mouth.

"Well done, son!" his mother shouted.

Their son, however, had a different opinion on the subject. I watched his blond hair. To be honest, I wasn't much interested in it. I was watching the changes in his eyes, where stallions neighed and kicked, and sparks flew. I loved fighting stallions and sparks in a guy's eyes.

"Twenty five levs per barrel, but you'll put the sandals on my feet for me!" Rosko said, his eyes ablaze.

"Are you crazy?" the railway station roared to her son. "Her father, the nasty squirt, has more than thirty barrels. We'll lose heaps of money! You might as well be hung for a sheep as for a lamb and—"

"Shut up, woman! Your son is speaking," Rosko's father cut her short. "I'm proud of you, my boy! Let Nettles bow down before you and put the sandals on your feet!"

I bent forward to pick up the sandals. If you scraped the dust from Rosko's feet and collected it, it could fill their bungalow halfway to the roof. I didn't look at the dust, though. I concentrated on his legs, I stroked his ankles, and I did that very gently. Then I caressed his toes, although I couldn't see clearly which toe I touched, the dust was so thick.

"What are you doing, viper?" Rosko shouted. Wasn't I surprised! I thought he'd smile at me, but what did he do? He called me names instead.

"Can't you see what I'm doing? Your feet are covered with mud and grime. You haven't washed them since you trod on well-rotted manure in your cowshed last week."

"We don't have a cowshed. I've been plowing the fields."

"Never mind. I thought I could wipe your feet first. Otherwise, you'll make your sandals dirty."

"Let your father know one thing, Nettles," Rosko's mother barked. "If the squirt harms a hair on my son's head while he's working for you, I'll, well ..." The woman gnashed her teeth. "I'll trap him and I'll flay him alive."

"Nettles is much worse than her father!" Rosko's father chipped in. "Nettles, if your brothers pester my son, I'll cut their noses off. Do I make myself clear?"

"Uncle Stancho, listen. I'd like to offer you something. I'll stay in your house while Rosko scrapes the barrels. I'll be held hostage. Aunt Dobra and I will sit in the kitchen, talking. "

"Talking? To you? I can't stand you," the woman said.

"Why not?" Rosko's father said. "Let her stay in our kitchen and Rosko will be safe enough. She'll pay him in the evening. He scrapes, let's say, three barrels, she gives him the money. Fair's fair. Then your wine will smell of naked girls, Nettles." He spat on the linoleum.

"Fair's fair," I agreed. "Short reckonings make long friends. One should always be honest with people."

"As honest as vipers can be," Rosko's father remarked.

"She could be as mad as a hatter for all I care," his mother said smugly. "The important thing is she'll pay. She can go jump in the lake after that."

"Give me an advance of ten levs," Rosko said suddenly. "I want ten levs now."

I had a hundred lev bill in my pocket but I never offered anybody an advance. I hated doing that.

"I have no penny to bless myself with," I said. "And I tell you the truth."

"Then leave your sweatshirt here. I'll take it instead of an advance," his mother said.

"I'm ready to give you my sweatshirt, Aunt Dobra, but I have no clothes under it. I'll have to go back home naked," I said.

"I don't give a damn about you naked or not," Rosko declared. "Leave your shoes here. You can go back home barefoot."

I took off my shoes and left them in front of his mother.

"Rosko, you come tomorrow at 6 a.m. to my father's wine-cellar," I said. "So long." I took the narrow road home, which ran parallel to the river.

Never in my life had my feet touched softer dust. I had never been so happy since the day in my childhood when Dad bought me a kite. I had worked hard for it. I sold all our lettuce at the marketplace in Pernik at a price twice higher than the one Dad had set. I remembered I felt like a million dollars; quite a crowd thronged to buy my merchandise. I could sell those guys nettles instead of lettuce. It was not the profits that made me happy. I was walking on air because I saw the way the guys looked at me. If a woman couldn't sell her merchandise at a good price then she'd better go and clean her cattle-shed while I sold lettuce to her husband.

On the following day I went to my father's wine-cellar. I knew Rosko was there. I immediately picked out the barrel in which he worked. The sounds of his scraping made the air in the room bristle.

"Rosko," I said. He didn't answer me.

My workers arrived as dawn broke and I gave each one of them a fiver.

"It's my birthday today," I lied to them. "Go and drink a beer to my health. You can drink some yellow brandy, too. Don't come back before noon."

The yellow brandy was most abominable, indeed. I suspected Dad brewed it from rotten tomatoes. I sold the concoction at daybreak when the night shift workers came back to the village on their jangling bus.

"The viper has put on a dress that hides nothing of her," someone said. I couldn't care less. The yellow brandy sold like hot cakes. They ogled me and they leered at me. I didn't try to stop them. What the hell! Their eyes couldn't bite my skin sore, could they?

"Rosko, can you hear me?" I shouted.

He stopped scraping. It occurred to me he had stopped smelling of cows. I wondered how, knowing that even the roof tiles in their house smelled of cows.

"Rosko, can you hear me?"

"What do you want?" He didn't stop working with his chisel.

"Stop scraping, please. I'd like to make you an offer."

He scraped on assiduously.

"Rosko, will you marry me?"

I couldn't tell you what happened exactly. Perhaps he dropped the hammer and it hit his toe, or he simply stomped around the bottom of the barrel. If my father was here, he'd give Rosko a piece of his mind. Dad hated it when somebody ruined his wine barrels.

"Now Rosko, try to concentrate and don't drop the hammer on your toes again," I advised him. "If you marry me, I'll make Dad give you the wine-cellar." It was so quiet that I could hear the sun crawl on the roof tiles. "If the cellar is not enough for you, I'll give you the two stallions: Whitey and Black, you know them. They are mine and I can give them to anyone I want."

"Go away!" he thundered from inside the barrel, and his hammer and chisel went to work again.

"Calm down, please. You'll ruin the barrel and then Dad will shoot you with his gun. Even I'll do that if you ruin that barrel."

"Go away, snake!" Rosko roared.

"Does that mean yes?" I asked him. "I didn't quite get your meaning."

134

"I won't marry you even if your father gave me the wine cellar, the smithy, the wheat fields, Whitey and Black, his car and the bed he sleeps in."

"Are you sure?" I asked. "I don't make an offer like that every day."

"Listen what, you cow! You are lucky I am in the barrel. If I wasn't, I'd slap you across the face. Do I make myself clear now?"

He did, and if he wasn't in the barrel, I'd spray my hair conditioner in his eyes. It was true I was good at enduring insults, but I wasn't that good. Rosko's luck was up today. I imagined the stallions fighting in his eyes and I saw the sparks fly under their hooves. I thought to myself, You don't know me, Rosko. I'll show you.

"Okay," I said, taking myself in hand. "You are unwilling to marry me, I understand. Wouldn't you like to kiss me at least? I sent all the workers to the pub and gave them money for two gallons of yellow brandy. There's no one in the cellar but you and me."

"What?" His hammer hit the bottom of the barrel with a dull thud.

"Look," I said, "if you drop anything in that barrel once again, I'll dump a bucket of slops onto your head. I have the bucket ready at hand. What would you say to my proposal?"

"Every time I look at you I feel like puking."

"It's dark in the barrel. You couldn't look at me even if you wanted to," I said. "In case you can see in the dark, I'll blindfold you. What do you say to that?"

I didn't wait for his answer.

I had prepared a ladder beforehand; Dad and my brothers used it when they thrashed the big walnut tree behind the sheep pen. Rosko had used that ladder, too, to climb up and get into the barrel.

"Go chase yourself!" he called out.

"It's too late," I said.

I clambered up the ladder and jumped into the barrel. Rosko tried hard to protect himself. He put up his hands to ward me off, then violently pushed and jostled me. It was impossible to shove me out. A barrel, unlike a bus, had no doors, so he couldn't kick me out.

There was another thing; I was good at loving guys. It was as easy as shelling peas and selling lettuce at the marketplace in Pernik. The night shift workers called me "grass snake" and "Nettles", but they drank gallons of my yellow brandy all the same. I could sell any man the dust his wife had collected in her vacuum cleaner while she hoovered the kitchen floor.

"Go away! Go oh … away aw … Oh!" Rosko could say no more.

I did the most natural thing to him. I kissed him. In the beginning, Rosko tried to repulse my attacks, but soon he became aware that I wished him well. He calmed down and let me do what I had planned. It felt good. It felt fabulous, and I liked it the way I liked the silver kite Dad had bought me in my childhood. The barrel felt warmer than the dust on the road the other day. I was so happy I stroked the staves twice although they were grimy with the dregs.

"My God!" Rosko whispered.

I saw him stroke the barrel, too.

"Do you want me to blindfold you?" I asked him.

"Yes," he said

"But I'll have to tear my blouse. Will you buy me a new one?"

"Uh-uh."

"What does that mean? Yes or no?"

"I'll buy two blouses for you, you cow!"

"What? What did you call me? Cow?"

I was convinced cows were good-natured and noble animals. If Rosko had called me 'snake,' I wouldn't have taken offence. I was a snake in the grass and I couldn't do anything about it.

Even when we were in the sixth grade, I noticed how Rosko's eyes gleamed beautifully. He used to walk home after school and I followed him, heaving deep sighs. I loved Rosko so much I thought I'd die for him. Fifteen years later, I knew love was not love if it made a girl die for a guy or trot after him like a horse. Love happened best in a wine barrel. The guy cleaned the dregs and scraped the staves for you, and besides, he wasn't able to kick you out because, as I mentioned before, a barrel has no doors.

"It was great! Oh boy!" Rosko breathed.

"It was not a boy, it was me," I told him.

He said again, "Oh boy! Oh boy!" An hour later, and soon after that I climbed out of the barrel.

"Look here," I said as I reached for the bucket of slops I had prepared beforehand in case he kept on calling me names. "Rosko, there are many more barrels to scrape. I'll bring you boiled eggs, honey and sausages in the morning. That sort of food will make you very strong. I know that from experience. You remember Petarcho? That was the guy who took to drinking after he broke up with me."

"You've got a nerve speaking about Petarcho, cow!" Rosko thundered from inside of the barrel.

I had given a pledge that if he called me once again the name of that useful animal, I'd pour the slops on his head, and so I did. I ran the risk of ruining Dad's reputation of a vintner. His wine might lose its fragrance of naked girls. It could acquire a different smell.

"I'll kill you!" Rosko shouted then took to swearing. In these parts, we believed that if a man didn't cuss, he was seriously ill.

"Rosko, be careful," I warned him. "I'll drop another bucket onto your head."

"Cow slut!"

I didn't hesitate for a moment. I hurled the empty bucket at him and left the wine cellar, its thick stone walls muffling the sound of his voice. That was good, for I wasn't that keen on being told what kind of a bitch I was.

On the following morning, I slipped into the next wine barrel. My father had marked the thing with a white cross, so Rosko knew which barrel he was to scrape that day. At 7 a.m. he crept into my barrel, not suspecting I was waiting for him.

At a certain point, both of us must have fallen asleep right there – sprawled full length across the bottom of the barrel, the boiled eggs and the sausages I had brought scattered around us.

"Son! Son, you look done in! You'll become a hard drinker! That Nettles bitch! She's already ruined Petarcho." I was awoken by a string of raucous, wild shouts. Rosko stirred by my side.

Somebody was shining flashlights and lanterns in our faces. I saw my father, clutching the big petroleum lamp with which he illuminated the room for the newborn colts in the stable. I saw Rosko's mother, too. She played the powerful torch over the two of us. I remembered I had seen her carry that torch when she came back from work at night, climbing up the hill to their house.

"She'll ruin him for sure, that bitch!" That was Stancho, growling. His voice sounded far away from our cozy barrel.

"Stancho, wait a minute!" my father yelled.

"Hey, squirt!" Rosko's mother yelled back. "I hope you'll fork over enough money to make us keep our mouths shut about what we saw. Why should we wait for you?"

"Wait for me to bring my gun to shoot you and your husband with," my father said. "You've just called my only daughter a bitch. I could hear that clearly."

"She is a bitch all right!"

"Dobra," my father said calmly. "Don't forget one thing, I'll make you pay for the bullets I'll shoot through your ass. Mark my words."

"She's a bitch! Yes, she is a bitch!" Dobra insisted.

Rosko hid his chest with my skirt. His skin glistened like a wet quince in the light of my father's petroleum lamp.

Suddenly Rosko sat up and shouted, "She's not a bitch! Galla is the most kind-hearted girl I have ever met!"

"What?" they all roared in unison.

"What did you say?" Dad muttered.

"I …" Rosko started. At that moment, I wasn't looking at him, but I knew that the stallions kicked and jumped in his eyes, and sparks flew under their hooves. These were magnificent sparks. I was sure they could set fire to the wine cellar.

The flashlights and the lamps burned in my eyes, making me itch all over. But I felt like a million dollars. No one had ever said I was the most kind-hearted girl he knew in the world.

"I can't live without her!" Rosko yelled.

The wine barrel thundered so powerfully that the iron hoops, which kept it bound together, shook and pealed like church bells. Dad, or maybe Rosko's father, had given them a kick.

THE SIXTEENTH FLOOR

Sanya darted up the stairs, a floor or two above her she heard hasty tramping. Ivan! She called out, but the shoes dashed faster, pattering towards the top floor of the block of flats. Her son ran like mad. Filled with panic, she rushed after him. Why was that six year old kid fleeing to the sixteenth floor? She already tracked him down twice on this very staircase. He was a small, silent boy, quiet on his chair while Sanya watched the newscast on the TV. He didn't eat much and quietly lost weight in his corner since his father went away. The worst thing was he now ran again, in his old bedraggled sweater, to the ugly sixteenth floor. Perhaps he wanted to see the Struma River that stole like a cat under the bridge, or he planned to stare at the hill overgrown with prickly bushes and mushrooms. He'd done that several times.

"Ivan!"

At last the pounding shoes stopped.

"Mom," his voice sounded soft and that threw her into panic. She imagined him standing in front of an open window on the top floor, just as the other day when he hurled her new jacket from the balcony of their apartment.

"Why did you do that?" she had asked.

"Because of you," her son had said." It's your fault." Then he had rushed again to the sixteenth floor.

"Ivan!" Sanya shouted. His silence made her freeze in her tracks. She had worried herself sick in vain. Ivan waited, bristling, squatting on the floor. "What?" she asked him. He didn't answer. That annoyed her. His silences gave her pounding headaches. Now she saw her son had thrust his hand under his scruffy sweater.

"What have you got in your hand?" Sanya asked, feeling a nest of pain kick between her eyebrows. "Let me see it."

Her son, who looked so much like Pavel, his father, cowered at her feet. He stayed as silent and watchful as Pavel, and one day would follow in his footsteps and go away. She was sure of that. "Okay, what's in your hand?"

Her son lay on his stomach, his scrawny chest burying his hand in which he hid something. She looked through the window; he had just chucked out one of her blouses, the orange one that had become entangled in the branches of the walnut tree under their block of flats.

"Why?" she asked, knowing the boy wouldn't answer. A month ago, he had started growling, quietly, like a wolf-cub, when he thought she was not at home. Her son slept, dressed in Pavel's T-shirt. Sometimes in the evening, the kid wailed obstinately, crouching by the wardrobe where some of his father's clothes had remained.

"Let me see your hand," Sanya said.

Unexpectedly, the boy stretched out his fist. He often did that. He gripped something in his fingers and stood silent, his hand outstretched. If she asked a question the kid growled.

This time he unclenched his fist and a note slipped through his fingers. It was a crumpled piece of paper, so tattered that she had no idea where he had taken it from. Then she knew.

Her son had torn it out of the calendar, from the month of April. It was the month of headaches, of colds and bad memories. On all the dates of April, and on the picture of the running children, her son had scrawled in block letters that were as big as the spring: Let it rain a lot.

"Why should it rain a lot?" Sanya asked. She expected no response. The kid answered her questions after a couple of hours, sometimes after a day. He spoke, wrapping himself in Pavel's blankets. Perhaps he talked to his father's T-shirt.

This time Ivan said, "I want it to rain".

Ivan still had not learned to write some of the letters at school and she wondered why he bothered to print them on the picture of the running children. She was surprised he had answered her.

"Dad comes home when it rains."

"Yes," she said.

It was true. Pavel had returned home twice and it had been raining all the time. She left her room and waited in the rain, under the walnut tree, while Pavel talked to the boy.

Sanya could not live with lies — she knew sometimes men fell in love with another woman and went crazy about her. Such a thing could not happen to Pavel, she believed. Yet it happened. She had no idea if that

140

woman had gone away, or Pavel's love for her had died, but he came back home.

Sanya could not stand by his side. Her nose bled. Perhaps it was on account of the smell. Pavel smelled of betrayal after that woman. The thought that he had sunk down into the armchair in which she sat now made her growl. Perhaps her son had learned that from her.

"Why do you go to the sixteenth floor?" she asked.

"Because of the rain," her son said. "I'll leave this note to the sky. It will know I want it to rain. I learned the letters "N' and "T" and wrote the note."

"Okay," Sanya said. "Leave the note here. I hope it will rain, son."

"But you don't want dad to come back home," the boy muttered.

Suddenly, Sonya made up her mind. She could not stand Ivan dashing to the top floor any more. She'd been worried sick. She just couldn't live through it once again.

"Ivan," she started. "I wish it would rain now. I'll write a note to the sky, too."

"Are you lying to me?" Ivan whispered, but his face relaxed. She didn't know what to say. The kid took her hand, pulled it and said, "Then let's go."

She wanted to tear another sheet from the calendar, the one with the month of May, but her son insisted, "I'll have to wait a long time if dad comes in May. Please, write you want it to rain in April."

In the afternoon, Sanya and the boy went to the sixteenth floor again. Its ceiling knew all the clouds of the town. The sky lived above the satellite antenna on their block of flats. Sanya wrote in her handwriting as round as a string of mushrooms, "Let it rain a lot."

"Why did you throw out my jacket and my blouse?" she asked her son. "You know they are expensive and we don't have much money."

"I know," Ivan answered. She expected he'd lapse into silence, squatting in front of Pavel's bed. Suddenly he said, "You put your jacket in dad's wardrobe. It doesn't belong there."

"It's not true," Sanya said. Her nose bled when her clothes remained in that wardrobe. Her nose bled even when she sat in the armchair in which he had reclined. She could have sold it, that ancient armchair, but she paid two guys to set fire to it instead, and waited all the time, staring

141

at the flames. Then she bought a big bottle of brandy for the guys who burnt Pavel's place in her mind. She drank with them. She drank so much she could not talk after that. Perhaps her voice had turned into a coal after the armchair disappeared.

She felt no hatred for that woman, she managed to keep a level head when she received letters from her, filled with requests for small favors. But when she saw her husband's forgotten shirt, his book, or his shoes her arms tingled and went dead. She struggled to forget him, but the blood, which spurted from her nose, could not forget.

"You are bad when you wear that jacket and blouse," her son said. "When you put them on it doesn't rain. Dad can't come home. I'd rather stay with him than with you."

"Is that why you threw out my clothes?" Sanya asked. Her son did not say anything as he pressed the month of April to his chest. The three of them: the boy, his mother and April climbed up the stairs to the sixteenth floor where the sky lived above the enormous satellite antenna.

"There we go," Sanya said and glued the sheet from the calendar to the window which faced the clouds. The boy checked if the note was firmly affixed to the glass, then his mother and he went home, and the month of April remained on the roof to wait for the rain.

Then the boy fell asleep. He was in Pavel's T-shirt, the only one that had remained in their flat. Sanya had soaked it for a week in washing powders to kill Pavel's smell, but Pavel stayed on.

Sanya took the cellular phone and dialed a number, the number that made her ill. She prayed that nobody would answer, but Pavel's voice asked, "Is that you, San?"

"Yes, it's me," she said. His voice was anxious to learn more but she didn't want to listen to it. She was careful not to pronounce his name. Pavel used to bring her spring and warm rains until that woman's letters came.

"I want you to come when it begins to rain," Sanya said.

"I'll come right away," the telephone number offered and suddenly spring birds nested in it.

"No, come when it starts raining, please," that 'please' scorched her lips worse than the flames that had killed the old armchair.

Definitely, the antenna had called for the rain through its satellite channels. Even on the following day a torrential downpour hit the gnarled walnut tree that had been watching the Struma River for years and was perhaps as old as its waters. Sanya's orange blouse was sopping wet, a piece of the sun hopelessly entangled in the branches and the nest of sparrows, a garment that made her bad as Ivan had remarked. The rainier the sky became, the happier beamed her son's face.

She had prepared herself for that rain.

Even Ivan had noticed that.

"You've put on your green blouse, Mom. You are good when you have it on. But where's your pair of blue jeans? You cook delicious chicken soups when you wear it."

Sanya was ready. The pair of jeans, which cooked soup so well, had been neatly folded together with other clothes, and waited on the backseat of her old Fiat.

It was raining hard and her son hung around the front door, humming softly a song about red-haired pirates. His room had not heard of such a thing for a year. The rain found its way and flowed into the boy's happy face. The doorbell rang at last.

"I knew it," Ivan shouted. "I knew that the rain would bring him home."

Pavel came in. He was tall and handsome, but she felt dizzy. That was a sign that her nose would bleed. She had to control herself.

"I'm glad you came," Sanya said.

"Are you?" he appeared not to believe it. "Really?"

Ivan seemed to believe his mother for she had put on her good green blouse.

"Take a seat," Sanya said to Pavel. "I'll make the two of you some tea." She went to the kitchen and put the kettle on. In the kitchen, she did not feel giddy, but when she came back to Pavel, her arms tingled. Betrayal had a peculiar characteristic: it made her fingers tremble. "I've cooked chicken soup; there's no bread at home," she added. "You are probably hungry."

The boy's face burned like the flames that had eaten into the old armchair and made her get drunk.

"I'm glad you take care of us," Pavel told her.

"This happened because of the month of April, which we glued to the window," the boy murmured happily. His father did not understand that but ruffled his hair all the same.

"I'll go and buy bread," Sanya said. She did not allow her nose to bleed. She pushed the blood back where it belonged.

"I'll go," Pavel offered.

"I'll go, Mom," her son chimed in. "This green blouse of yours is so good today."

Sanya took the shopping bag.

She waved at them and went out of the room. She had prepared herself. She passed by the bakery and padded across the street to the old Fiat. There, on the backseat, her clothes waited: her T-shirts and the pair of jeans which cooked well.

She had left her son with his father and the month of April, glued to that window.

MONIKA

Monika never haggled over the price of the brandy she bought. She took the bottle, threw the money on the table and that was all. The people in these parts lived on the brandy they sold her, survived like the grass-snakes, sticking to the stones and the brown soil that yielded only evil hot peppers and potatoes. Hawthorns, blackthorns and damson trees throve on the wild rocky slopes and if you picked their small fruits you made that yellow brandy that Monika was interested in. The folks raised their children on the money from their demijohns, on wild plums and the sun. The moon didn't give birth to days but to yellow brandy, wild and wicked, smelling of parasol mushrooms, and rattling with the noises ravens made as they spread their wings.

Monika didn't bargain with the guys from the village of Staro. They were skinflints and their shadows reeked of fights and unpaid debts. She drove her ramshackle van to Staro through the knee-deep mud and the holes in the dirt roads.

She hated all the villagers, but knew she had to put up with one of them, Stoyko. He had two little sons, wild like eels, agile and taciturn, yet he regularly took Monika to one of the empty houses on the periphery of the village. Stoyko had a wife as well, a pale, silent shadow that climbed the hills, picking haws and sloes for the brandy. That woman sucked tomatoes out of the sand and planted cherry trees in between crags and rocks, stunted, undersized saplings that grew there in spite of the savage heat. Monika had seen her many times drag huge tin cans full of duck-weedy water to her cherry trees. There were some puddles, miserable remnants of the river, which didn't run dry in summer.

In summer, Stoyko brought Monika to that derelict house; many of the houses remained ownerless if you didn't count the old dogs that outlived their masters. There, amidst the ancient rugs and bleached photographs of mustachioed men, women and flocks of children, Monika and Stoyko made love. Monika didn't know what Stoyko did to make the men in shabby trousers sell her their brandy cheap. Perhaps it was his ill temper that at times scared her, or maybe they did it because he dug the graves for their deceased relatives for a very modest fee. In return for a loaf of white bread, Stoyko dug a most wonderful grave, deep and comfortable and dead folks joined their maker without a hitch. Perhaps their maker was not very keen on that village, some suspected.

They had stones instead of land in their gardens, but then stones were useful, too. Snakes mated under them. The children here became rocks and snakes from an early age. They drank their fathers' brandy which smelled of ravens, clouds and stolen pine trees. For fuel, men hewed the pines furtively, at night. The plundered hillsides, denuded of trees, shone like bones and produced toadstools. Snakes slept under their flat heads; lizards, thick like ropes, ate them until unexpectedly the sky exploded and started dumping rains on the potato fields.

Rain after rain and no break for two months until the river was born again. It rushed, rumbling, sweeping roots and bushes, wrenching sand from beneath the sitting rooms of the houses. The water dragged along drowned snakes and lizards and Monika remembered it had mixed with the brandy in the demijohns. Then the river smelled of pines and ravens, the brandy was the color of dead snakes, but she and Stoyko were very happy in that ownerless house in spite of the downpour. Everything around them was wet and Monika wondered if the puddles on the floor were water or brandy. She had seen Stoyko's wife in the mud, erect like a lamppost under the rain, watching.

Monika chose Stoyko for two reasons: the thick brandy, and because most of the other villagers were old men who did not look at her the way Stoyko did. At times, she thought of his sons. Last year they went to school by bus, then they had to walk, for petrol was too expensive. Children here were like the fish in the river that ran dry, a true rarity. Unlike the fish, the water snakes learned to live on dry land and mated with the real snakes. Thousands of them were born and swam in the rain. When Monika drove the brandy to Pernik, she smelled of pines, of mushrooms and snakes.

In the beginning, she sold it in the main square, squatted down behind a makeshift stall, an ancient table. She had pilfered it from an old house whose landlord was a feeble mutt. Monika managed to always push up the price, then checks started and inspectors wanted to see her permit, which she didn't have. So she rented a cellar from Nenko, a mechanic who could make a car out of an old vacuum cleaner if he was not too drunk. Monika paid him the rent in brandy but not the one that smelled of swelling rivers. She gave him a glass of the hogwash brew she bought from the gypsies in the village of Vladimir. These gypsies made brandy out of cabbage leaves and turnips, or maybe they used cinders to produce their concoction. One often had headaches and one's mug became blue after drinking it. Nenko's mug, however never became blue, he felt no pain and was quite comfortable with the Vladimir brew she gave him. He told her once, "I'd die for you." But he could not love when drunk. He only made broken boneshakers good again.

Monika sold her brandy in thick opaque glasses she had pinched from the house of the old mutt. A disordered line of men, bluish in the face, formed down the flight of stairs to her cellar. The men downed the Vladimir brandy contentedly for she sold it dirt cheap. When Monika remained in the mechanic's cellar for a week, Stoyko arrived in Pernik to visit her. She could only guess how much he had squandered to reach Pernik. He rushed to her cellar and thundered, "Where's the other guy?"

He was spoiling for a fight with the men from the line because, in his view, Monika probably cheated on him. She locked and bolted the door then she made love to him while the guys waited humbly for her to open the cellar again. They desperately wanted their thirty-five cent glass of Vladimir. Stoyko could hardly bear them all the same.

"Let's run away to Spain," he told Monika. "We'll plant damson trees there, we'll distill brandy and we'll make the Spaniards look blue in the face like us. Or you come back home and stay with me."

In Pernik, there were no clients for the thick brandy with the sun and clouds in it, but Monika enjoyed its yellow presence behind her back. There was the river, the mushrooms and Stoyko's two sons in its amber depths. Monika had seen the boys write swear words on her van. Once, they punctured all its four tires with nails and the van lay down on the road like a dead cow. Then Monika watched the father thrash the kids with a stick he snapped off from the stunted cherry tree his wife had planted. It looked as if he had hit them with the tin-cans the scrawny woman had dragged in the scorching heat of July. The boys had not tried to evade the blows, their eyes fastened on their mother's face. When Stoyko was gone they threw stones and cow dung at Monika. Strange, Monika was out of sorts on account of that woman who didn't do anything but stick out from the ground like the goal in the empty football field. An open goal that nobody cared for, that was what that woman was. Monika felt sorry for her, but not so much as to give her a bill from the bundle she had in her pocket after she sold the Vladimir brandy.

She felt sorry because her own mother lived alone in one of the houses beneath the Black Peak. Her father had moved in with a young woman Monika liked and played backgammon with from time to time. Monika's mother was sparing of words, her face closed like a wall. Perhaps her father was right, he moved in with Darina. Darina who smoked like a brick field, sang pop hits, jumbling up tunes and rhymes in a hot unbearable mess. She sold vegetables in the market square in Pernik and her mouth never ceased babbling even if she had a cigarette in it. Monika's father listened to her, smiling, happy that he could hear a human being speak. When his second wife shut up to light another cigarette, her father's face looked worried.

When Monika was little, her mother chased the boys away from their backyard. The girls were afraid of her, too, because of the wall she had instead of a face. If Monika wanted to kiss a boy she had to walk to the neighboring village. Rumors had it Monika's mother dabbled in black magic. Actually, all she had done was to buy a cheap plastic icon to which she prayed day and night, petitioning for her daughter to become rich. Monika's mother was taciturn, but her power of speech broke down completely when she found her husband with a woman, their neighbor of many years. The man had simply called in for a chat, but the woman's words had plunged into his heart and he had kissed her. Monika's mother lapsed into silence and neighbors said it was not an accident that toadstools sprouted up in her backyard, slugs infested her garden, and under the ground the moles were so many they ate even the rocks. It was only the brandy in her house that was really good.

One day, Yani came to buy brandy from Monika's cellar. In fact, she came to know his name was Yani much later, when he paid for a gallon of the sickening brew from Vladimir and started drinking it mulishly, his back propped against the wall, tears welling up in his eyes. His face became blue, even his black eyes turned blue and Monika feared he might breathe his last in her cellar.

"Why are you doing this?" Monika asked him, noticing that in spite of his livid complexion the young man was as handsome as an angel. He had dark hair and a face that appeared like a prayer to her, the face she had been dreaming of while her van got stuck in the mud of the dirt roads. She had seen that face while Stoyko groaned he'd do anything she wanted, forgetting it was raining and that drowned grass-snakes floated down the river. Yani's dark drunk tears dripped into the cheap brew from Vladimir as Monika kissed him.

"She's gone," the lad muttered.

Monika asked him what his name was and he didn't know. Monika had been dreaming all her life that someone would forget his name because of her, but that never happened. Her own name was notorious in the whole district and when villagers saw her van, she knew they said, "The leech will be here again." Women substituted her name with other insulting words and Stoyko's wife was said to be seized by a fit beside the pot of soup she cooked, if one of her sons mentioned Monika's name by mistake.

Monika took out the lad's wallet and his identity card told her his name was Yani. She kissed him again and slammed the door in the noses of the men who waited for her brandy in a quiet line. They were soft-spoken and one might presume they were in a church or waited in front of a surgeon's office. Sometimes Monika awarded a 'Vladimir' to the most tractable one among them. A Vladimir meant a free beer-bottle of the gypsy brew. The lucky man who got it swept the floor and smiled at Monika. She watched him closely, fearing he could pinch one of her precious opaque glasses. Although the door was locked, Yani did not stop drinking and sobbing while Monika kissed him. He looked so beautiful, Monika made up her mind to give him a bottle of her true amber brandy. It was all August mornings, damsons and warm winds. The damson trees sucked life out of the crags and infused rocks into her brew. There was gold in the hills, and surely it squeezed its way into her demijohns.

Monika gave Yani the best of her amber treasure for she admired his chest so much. She had never been so impressed before, not even when her mother gave her a pair of green cords. Then the villagers wondered if it was really Monika, or some pretty girl from Pernik who had lost her way and chased the wind amidst the snakes and lizards in their backyards. Monika's mother remained in her room, silent like the dead grass on the hills.

One day Monika discovered her mother had a mania for building a wall around her house. Her neighbors kept away from her even when she went to buy bread, so the woman started piling up rocks round her backyard. She dragged stones, thorns, and stray brambles that were welcomed by the lizards. When Monika came to see her mother, she lit up, if it was possible for a wall to light up. Her mother hugged her and Monika wondered how that woman survived there in the sun. The cherries had withered, the peppers had become dry like flint and the moles had turned the garden into a wasteland of craters and molehills. Her mother had a nanny-goat named Hope, a bitch named Hope, too, an old TV set and a calendar. Every time Monika visited her, the heap of stones around the house was larger, Monika wondered over her mother's sanity.

"How's your mother?" her father asked, taking a guilty look at the heat in her backyard. "They say she's off her head."

"She is okay," Monika said.

Once she found her mother talking to a young man whose face was much different from Yani's. That man's face was no icon and cried for no girl that was gone. That man was blond, colorless, and thin like the withered tomato branches behind the house. He constantly dug the garden and planted beans, looking more and more like the moles to which he talked in a soft, imploring voice. He spoke to Hope, the bitch, and to Hope, the nanny-goat, and her mother listened, smiling. Her mother appeared happy she could hear a living thing speak. Then her mother asked the scraggly man to tell her fairy tales in the evening. Monika was rendered speechless. She didn't think much of his tales, yet she started to suspect she fancied the man. She gave him some of her amber brandy, a teacup, and asked him to come and catch grass-snakes under the stones with her. People gossiped, said that her mother caught grass snakes and baked them to cure her silence and aching knees with their skins. The blond man took a gulp of yellow thunder of Monika's brandy and his transparent face became purple right away. "What did you do to him!" her mother cried out, terrified.

That purple face told Monika the blond one was not a real man and had most probably visited her mother to have his body cured with grass snake's skin. Monika left the two of them alone. She stopped asking herself why that scrawny guy had crawled behind the pile of stones and thorns, surrounding her mother's backyard. Monika's mother had cured him for a month before his face healed and became again white and soft like a girl's. One evening, Monika found the two of them sitting in front of a bucket of milk. Hope, the bitch, sniffed at a heap of snake's raw meat. Hope, the nanny-goat, bleated softly. It was pouring with rain and animals and people were in the sitting room.

It was autumn, the best time to buy brandy in these parts. So many toadstools had sprouted around the thorns and stones in her mother's backyard that Monika was scared. When she examined them carefully, she gasped. They all were edible mushrooms. The scrawny man and her mother drank milk and smiled at each other. That was so frightful and so amazing that Monika could not believe it. Some guys in the village said the man was a brandy merchant, but that was certainly not true: the only brandy merchant in the village was Monika.

"What's your name?" Monika asked the scrawny guy, but he did not answer. He had forgotten what his name was and sat there, smiling at her mother. Rain spurted out of the torn sky, but the blond one did not see it. He looked at her mother, not even telling her fairy tales. He looked at her and didn't know his name.

Yani, too, had forgotten his name because of a girl. After Monika locked the door of the cellar, she took him behind the only demijohn of yellow thunder. There she admired his magnificent face and loved him. He couldn't concentrate, though. He told her time and again about that girl. She was so beautiful that it stopped raining when she showed up. This made no difference to Monika. She loved him on the mat Stoyko had given her. Perhaps his wife had woven it years ago. Stoyko never forgot his name. He had grown wild and refused to drink the amber brandy. He was afraid he might fall asleep while he was with Monika. One day, after Monika had taken Yani to her amber-filled demijohn in the cellar, the rain stopped and someone knocked at the door. That had never happened before. No one was allowed to bang on Monika's door, not even Nenko, the mechanic she paid two Vladimir bottles a month. He drank his

Vladimir, cleaned the cobwebs in the cellar and swept the floor. Whoever he is, he'll pay through the nose, Monika thought and opened up.

A girl stood before her, such a pretty girl that the men who waited in an unsteady line suddenly sobered. Monika had not seen such a beautiful woman before, although women from the hills of the grass snakes and damson trees were usually pretty. Even Stoyko's wife was pretty when she jutted out like a sword, watching them from the backyard of the house.

"Go away!" Monika said to the girl. At that point she saw Yani's face light up. Yani's face, as beautiful as an icon that Monika had just kissed, glowed and smiled. The girl smiled as well, she smiled so thinly that the brandy in the demijohns throbbed. Monika's mother and the blond, colorless man had smiled at each other like that by the bucket with the milk. Yani rushed to the girl.

"Yani!" Monika shouted. "Yani!" but he had forgotten his name again.

When Monika drove back with the van to buy up the brandy in the village of Staro, she saw a thing that amazed her. Stoyko stood alone in the middle of his backyard, under a big bleached umbrella. "She went away with the children," Stoyko said to her.

His house looked exactly like it did two years ago, a low, one story building, its backyard swimming in the rain; no garden, just puddles and mud. The green tomatoes had rotted on their branches, decaying peppers, grey like the clouds, hung to the sodden ground. It was not necessary to plod their way to the house on the outskirts of the village. Monika moved in with Stoyko. His sons' school timetable was still glued to the wall; their old shoes and his wife's apron lay on the floor in the kitchen. On the first day, Stoyko collected the odds and ends and threw them out of the house. A new garbage heap had sprung up behind the rocks and branches Monika's mother had piled around her backyard. There, amidst the mushrooms that grew like mad, Stoyko dumped all that old junk. Stoyko and Monika didn't go out of the house for a whole week. One of the neighbors brought them food and drink from the village grocery store, ample supplies of bread, sausages and cheese. Love didn't happen when one was hungry.

The neighbor took care of them diligently because Monika had given him a pail of the thunder brandy. The man would have hauled the whole town of Pernik to them for a much smaller demijohn. Stoyko, wild with the brandy and Monika, smiled in his sleep. But he did not forget his name on account of her.

Then Monika bought up all the brandy from the villagers. She took the whole summer, the hills they had been tramping, their damsons, kernels and sloes. She bought the hours during which the men had strained their ears listening to the gurgling noises in the casks, waiting for the amber and thunder to trickle into the brandy still. She loaded up the van with the demijohns and was off to Nenko, the mechanic, who had already scoured and scrubbed the cellar for her. Its clean floor shone like a mirror, her regular clients had already fallen down the flight of stairs and waited for her, money in fists, ready for a Vladimir. When Monika drove back to the village of Staro, she saw a rusty chain and a padlock hanging on the front door of Stoyko's house. One of the windows had been boarded up. Behind it was the room where he had eaten a mountain of bread and sausages, and had made love happen as often as the raindrops in the rainstorm.

"Stoyko!" Monika shouted out. "Stoyko!"

Nobody answered her. The dog that had been hanging about the house while the neighbor took care of their food had vanished. A crumpled piece of paper was nailed to the wall. Some words were printed in pencil on the scrap. There were no commas, no full-stops, just enormous spaces, like toadstools, between the warped letters:

- k i d s a r e h u n g r y i a m w i t h

t h e ms t o y k o

The money Monika had made, the yellow rain, the rust of the chain on the door, weighed her down. She stood rigid, her lips stiff, her eyes cold and remote like the autumn wind.

MRS. BEEVA

I was carefully curling her thin hair that I had dyed from sickly blond to russet ginger more times than I could remember. I was using ancient silver rollers with the initials of the German company "Kipheuer-Witsch", her skull under my fingers as brittle as paper, her shoulders almost intangible under the heavy folds of her brocade dress that made her old skin twitch as I moved about her. It felt as if her soul was about to abandon her, disgusted with the silver rollers, loathing the brocade that weighed far more than the woman herself.

"My dear," she often addressed me, but I was neither dear nor hers. I felt the cold silver of Kipheuer-Witsch in her words. Her vowels were even and calm like an autumn day. Days and nights had blended into the smooth paste of her voice that told me about her husband, an eminent factory owner who had graduated in fine arts from the University of Vienna. A brilliant violin player, who had inherited his mother's sugar factories, an intellectual whom fate had tossed away in the insignificant country town, smelling of sweat and boredom, a settlement, which was bearable only in spring because at that time squalor was concealed under the blossoms of cherry trees. Her husband would play the violin in the evenings, she would listen to him and their little son would frolic by the fountains in the small park.

No, Mrs. Beeva would never allow the onus of the sugar factory to mutilate her heir's life; she despised the aroma of caramelized sugar, a poisonous transparent cloud that engulfed the whole town.

I couldn't care less about Mrs. Beeva's husband or her son. She had placed an advertisement in a local newspaper, in which I had wrapped my sandwich by accident: some cheese, tomatoes plus a baked pepper. The elderly lady wrote in her advertisement she would bequeath her gorgeous six-room apartment in the center of Sofia to the person willing to take care of her till death. There were eleven other women who were more than prepared to minister the old lady to her maker, for such a prize. To my amazement she made us all recite poetry. I had hated poetry all my life. Guys often tried to convince me that I had beautiful eyes and after I gave them what they wanted the prevailing number of them declared I was a slut. I wouldn't like to use the other vulgar word that guys called me now and then. You all know it, but I do not resort to obscenities even in my mind. Mrs. Beeva could hear my thoughts. Whenever words like "asshole" or "faggot" crept into my vocabulary, she fined me 100 Lev per each rude phrase. I could say farewell to my salary if I enjoyed three dirty expressions a month.

When I uttered an indecent part of the Bulgarian vocabulary Mrs. Beeva bristled up and her soul made best efforts to extricate itself from her thin hair and "Kipheuer Witsch" rollers. I knew what was at the roots of her troubles; she strongly suspected her son was gay. Actually, she not only suspected, her son Dennis had lived with a young man for seven years now. When Dennis visited his mother the two of them stood in front of the window overlooking the park with the broken swings, and wept. I couldn't tell you why they cried their hearts out. The truth was their pretty faces glistened in a profusion of tears. Her son had her exquisite shoulders that twitched exactly like Mrs. Beeva's, so I supposed his soul, too, was as sensitive and itchy as hers.

"My dear, he was a treasure," Ma'am explained to me most of the days while I combed her hair; she meant her husband. "Je l'adore," she told me in French and when I stared at her blank-faced, she heaved a deep sigh and translated the damned sentence for me, "I adore him." I couldn't care less, of course, but she made a habit of omitting 'Good Morning' and starting the day with "Je l'adore". Often she would ask me to open the mahogany chest of drawers. I had never imagined that a puny chest like that could be so expensive. She made me polish it with a special paste that her son brought from Vienna, and the poor mahogany wood shone with the energy of the moon and the sun combined. Actually, your ass would shine like the moon, too, if you polished it with that Vienna paste. My eyes hurt on account of the mahogany, but I polished the chest all the same. So, her husband, the treasure, played the violin every night— nocturne after nocturne, sonata after sonata until Mrs. Beeva felt blissfully happy. He kissed her good night to which she responded with a grateful smile, half asleep.

On the other hand, their son had a nurse, a young Mademoiselle, gentle and refined who recited Schiller in German, Byron in English and Baudelaire in French. The Mademoiselle could play the violin, the cello

156

and the pianoforte. She played different concertos so magnificently that Mrs. Beeva's son and husband wept silent tears by her side. Once in a blue moon Mr. Baev, when he was not utterly exhausted by the problems of the sugar factory, played the violin with the nurse and these were miraculous evenings, no doubt. What a pity that the lad asked his mother to hire a man to be his governess. Indeed, Dennis had no appetite at all, he pined and lost weight, he was such a delicate curly boy who recited Baudelaire in French and Schiller in German, but whenever Mademoiselle approached him and stretched across the table to touch his hand, the kid felt dizzy. If she remained in his room late in the night to read to him, then in the morning Dennis woke up covered in a horrible rash that mutilated his marble-white skin.

Before Mrs. Beeva reached the point where her son's marble skin was totally busted, I had usually managed to curl one third of her hair although it was as thin as laser rays. I knew what would come next. She wept, harassed by the memory of miserable Dennis and his ruined complexion. I gave her mineral water; she touched my hand, her skin always cold and icy. Perhaps death was already in her fingers and the chill came from the world beyond. It did not bother me, I was accustomed to touching death and obeying her usual order, "Go and clean my son's house, Monika."

I promptly promised I'd clean her son's and his boyfriend's houses, meanwhile thinking how I was to smuggle Miladin, a boy I slept with from time to time, into Mrs. Beeva's six-room flat. The walls of the flat were girded up for robberies; a thick network of black wires encompassed them. Ma'am had a safety system installed, which signaled the intrusion of gangsters, thieves, rapists, spiders, rodents and cockroaches by producing sounds of a differentiated pitch. Miladin always visited me wearing one of my dresses, so I told Mrs. Beeva he was our new charwoman. The charwoman was allowed to enter the flat twice a week. She cleaned its spacious six rooms furnished with Vienna divans, cabinets and tables from the eighteenth century. Mrs. Beeva was as good as blind without her glasses, so she asked to touch and check the charwoman's cheek—smooth skin was her obsession.

Maybe I had forgotten to mention that when Ma'am chose me among the eleven other competitors for the job, the first thing she did was to

157

touch my cheeks. She rejected professional nurses on the grounds they could not recite, they inadvertently blurted out impolite remarks or she thought their voices sounded ugly. I suspected the major reason she flunked them was that the skin of their faces did not feel smooth. She touched all cheeks in turn and selected me, because my skin is as smooth as a polished shoe. Quite apart from that I had succeeded in stammering out a whole stanza of Vazov's poem, *I am a Bulgarian*. Alas, that was a flash in the pan for later she made me recite Schiller and Shakespeare and I could not utter an articulate sound. I kept mum as if I was a dead fish. Yet I was the only one among the eleven competitors who knew these guys were poets, although I hated poetry. Mrs. Beeva said, "You are my girl," and I was.

Ma'am touched Miladin's cheek as well. He had fine bone structure and enormous blue eyes. I made him shave painstakingly before pouring French belle's perfume all over him. Mrs. Beeva adored French scents and unlike her eyes which made out you were not a cow but her servant, her nose differentiated between all the twelve different perfumes I spilt over Miladin. Sometimes she and Miladin wept together. She had somehow managed to move him with the story about the man she loved; that fortunate individual, of course, was not her husband, who in spite of all his accomplishments and undisputable qualities was 'simply a good friend'. The guy she was in love with was perfect. She had never used the word 'lover' when she described him, although he undoubtedly was a good one. O, what a shameful blemish that would be for his blessed heart and gentle soul. She adored him.

This blessed individual joined his maker on account of excessive consumption of alcohol, or maybe because he was one of the few drug addicts of his time. Whatever the truth, I often saw Miladin and Mrs. Beeva weep in unison for her beloved. Miladin sobbed most sincerely and Ma'am was sure he put his heart in his tears, although as I said before, her eyes were as good as if they had been gouged out. She had an eerie sixth sense of fakers and caught you on the spot if you but tried to trick her. I had made it a rule with Ma'am: better keep mum like a fried trout and let her touch your cheek than feign sincerity. I let her fingers on my cheek reminisce about her own beauty in her youth. She used to be a fascinating young minx, she said, and "My complexion was like yours at present, Monika". Somehow I couldn't make out the knot of silver rollers in her voice, which was accustomed to purchasing and selling, neither could I make out the tears in her thinning eyes.

I could play no musical instrument; I loathed violins, sonatas and nocturnes, but "God has blessed you with an angelic voice, my dear," Mrs. Beeva said and asked me to sing to her. I knew most of the hits of *Metallica*, but she shook uncontrollably whenever I attempted to sing them to her. She coerced me into cramming an Italian song and although I couldn't make heads or tails of what it said, I sang it to her, softly, so softly you could hear the clock knit the minutes into a rope around your neck. I crooned and cooed the Italian words until she began to weep, half of her hair captured in the rollers, the other half hanging like gossamer down her skull.

Miladin sat immobile on the piano stool in the antechamber. I often wondered how it was possible for his backside not to contract paralysis. But when I tucked Mrs. Beeva in and turned to look at him, I saw that his face was sopping wet.He did get upset about the song—Ma'am had translated it into Bulgarian for him. The song, of course, told a story about unrequited love. Miladin was so moved upon hearing it that he could not make love for a while. To be honest with you, a situation like that was highly frustrating for me. I hadn't given him my best dress to have him by my side soft like dough, teardrops all over him, while Mrs. Beeva snored in her mahogany bed.

I imagined what would happen if she discovered Miladin was not a woman. She might kick me out or might give Miladin the boot and keep me. Actually, I had chosen him on account of his ability to squeeze into my dress and look like a girl in it. I liked the blue look in his eyes, though.

One evening Beeva's son met Miladin who had dolled himself up in my dress. I expected some sort of disaster but Dennis remarked casually, "That is our new servant girl, isn't she?" and gave Miladin his old shirt as present. I should have smelled a rat back then.

As I curled the second half of Mrs. Beeva's hair, she would often tell me that, perhaps, it had been her fault that her son had developed the way he had. She knew very well that Dennis's skin blistered on account of his nurse's presence. So, one night when the lad pleaded with his mother, his eyes brimming with tears, to hire a boy to take care of him, she had given in. She had hoped that Dennis would get accustomed to man's company, learn to play man's games and behave like a man. Yet, it had the opposite effect. What a pity, Mrs. Beeva's husband said grieving over the beautiful night concerts with Mademoiselle. They could not recite together Schiller, Goethe and Heine any more. He could only bury his head in the heaps of sugar that his factory produced, and lament his days in the world of gruff workers and accountants who would bamboozle him into going bankrupt in a flash. Mademoiselle was so sorry, too ... an inordinately sensitive girl that no factory owner of repute would hire. Who else would want a lovesick nurse sprawling on the sitting room floor in your villa?

So the family hired a lad to take care of Mrs. Beeva's son. He was an exceptionally civilized young guy who recited William Blake and Hoelderlin, but, alas, his family went bust in the cruel crisis of 1940. That lad won everybody with his refinement, erudition and elegance and what a pity again! Several months after they hired him, Mrs. Beeva happened to search for her son's silk shirt in the wardrobe in his room. The thing she saw left her broken-hearted. Her son, already a young man himself, and his male nurse were naked together, God forgive me the obscene phrase I resorted to! For a fleeting instant Ma'am didn't know how she should react. If she announced her presence she could inflict a spiritual trauma on her son that wouldn't heal. She chose to circumspectly withdraw and on the very next day she asked her husband to fire the male nurse.

Mrs. Beeva's son fell into a black depression, then was hit by a crisis, a disease-like state during which he came up in an itchy rash. His marble skin looked like as if it had been covered with popcorns. He'd be okay, Mrs. Beeva told herself and made a firm decision—an act I could relate to the knot of clanging Kipheuer-Witsch silver rollers in her voice.

Another event, a more tragic one occurred soon after that. Her boy, Dennis, sold his books by Goethe, Schiller, Heine and all the rest of them. He pawned the presents he had received for his birthdays: a gold ring, a diamond, his horse La Rochefoucault, and even hawked several pairs of his shoes. Then Dennis rushed to seek for his male nurse. This romantic hunt had been in vain. Mrs. Beeva had prudently sent the individual to

160

Pirot, a town in Macedonia, to an asylum for aristocratic young men with psychotic disorders. At that point of the tale, the silver rollers curled Mrs. Beeva's voice into a wire that could strangle anyone. In the long run, the male nurse ran away from the asylum and embarked on a dangerous trip back to Bulgaria, begging for food and small change all the way down to Sofia, to his beloved Dennis, Mrs. Beeva's son.

Miladin had already heard that tale twice. The first time he listened to it his face was soaked with tears like a freshly irrigated lawn. Mrs. Beeva personally checked his cheeks and was deeply gratified by the charwoman's sympathy and good heart. Miladin was really upset; he remained soft almost half of the night, but as I had already pointed out, that could hardly be tolerated by me.

I convinced Mrs. Beeva we needed another charwoman, a more energetic one, and I substituted Miladin for another guy, a burlier one. He had a wiry beard, no matter he diligently shaved it, and when Mrs. Beeva touched his cheek she felt sorely disappointed. She declared that people who had suffered from small pox made her think of old age, varicose veins and wrinkles. Thus, Miladin came back, meeker than ever, and tried to convince me he had learnt his lesson well.

Whenever he wept, he dried his tears with a towel and made best efforts to conceal them from me. Alas, one day he recited "Freude, Schöne Göterfunken" by Schiller staring at a photograph in a silver frame, which showed Mrs. Beeva as a young woman of the beau monde. The old photo made it clear that Ma'am had just given birth to a most beautiful son smiling happily in his mother's arms. Actually, Miladin recited only the first stanza of *Freude*. He reiterated that absurd stanza muttering the German words like prayer every time he passed by Mrs. Beeva's photograph. She must have turned heads when she was young. It was the most logical thing that a beau should appear. At this point, I again eschewed the popular word 'lover'.

Every Tuesday and Thursday Miladin placed a red rose in front of Mrs. Beeva's photograph. Occasionally, he addressed me *Natalia* that was her personal name. In the beginning it really annoyed me, but when I saw that Natalia honed his skills, I let him call me the way he pleased. That didn't last long. On Thursday, before Miladin got his salary from

Ma'am, he most unexpectedly declared, "Ma'am, I am not a woman. I am a man. I admire your son. "Je l'adore!"

That sentence rendered us both speechless, awestruck.

No more do I curl Ma'am's hair using the ancient silver rollers with the initials of the German company Kipheuer-Witsch. That day she had them all buried in a big flowerpot. We purchased some soil from a park in Vienna for that flowerpot and her rollers. Now and then, she weeps tears of grief, letting them drop into the flowerpot, into the very heart of Kipheuer-Witsch.

NOT A SINGLE TREE

"That one!" Grandma Dora blurted out, chewing the sounds, her green eyes hot like tongs. I could not believe it; she hissed and bit the words like that when she thought of Boris. She had just come back from the front door, flushed and hot. Her blood pressure had probably reached her eyebrows and that meant death was stalking her by her easy chair. Death had been stalking grandma for eighteen years, ever since I introduced her to Boris. Since then, he had been "that one" who wanted to kidnap her only treasure, her granddaughter, on account of whom Grandma Dora made her best effort to go on living. She asked her Jewish gods to keep her whole and kicking so she could take care of me. She had lost my father, a wise thin man, and she had only me, plus two old friends, inveterate smokers, with whom she drank coffee. Occasionally, the two of them wept; not Grandma Dora. She drank vodka while her friends cried silent tears into their coffee cups.

"That one!" grandma repeated biting off several sounds. "I told him you were not available."

Our sons—Boris's and mine—were already grown. Grandma was happy they were at home, but they were "that one's" sons and when they fought she did not ask why; she knew. Staring at the air, foggy with feathers from their pillows after the fights, she snarled, "That one!" "You won't live with him under the same roof for a long time," she often remarked, even before Boris met "the other woman." Grandma Dora was convinced he'd clear out. When it would happen, was an issue of time and patience. "If you are so rattle-brained, I can't help you. You look at him as if he was a quiet November day, but he'll deceive you."

I met Boris under the chestnut trees in the school yard of the professional school for electricians in Radomir where I taught English, after my graduation from the university. The prospective electricians couldn't care less about English grammar; most of them were only interested in a learning a handful of obscene words. The present perfect tense was as remote a notion to them as tobogganing to me. Boris asked me if I had heard of a well-known local company I knew absolutely nothing about. Grandma Dora was right. I mooned about, stuffing my brain with obscure poetry or good-for-nothing novels. Boris was a physicist, a corporate manager or something, he said, but I wasn't listening, I could hardly wait for the end of the day. We didn't go to his room in the cheap hotel in Radomir. We didn't even go the motel five miles away from my school. Love happened quickly. There were chestnut trees, enormous ones that shone in the afternoon. The only thing I remember was how birds nestled under Boris's hands. On the following day after my classes and much present simple tense, chestnut trees sprouted up under his hands. Grandma Dora said, "He'll ruin your life, don't you see that? He's a liar, my girl, and you are my most precious thing."

"That one" gave me the sky with swallows and winds in it, with old whispers and the vodka, which grandma Dora drank. "He'd crush you like a nut and you're out of your mind. I can't help you. Have children then, have children. He'll go away for sure and the kids will remain with you."

My grandma drank her vodka carefully, for that was the medicine for her poor heart. Sometimes it pounded and thudded like the express train to Sofia, the same train that would take her to her friend, death. And yet Grandma loved my sons. "They are chestnuts and wasters like their father, but there is summer in them, too, and summer is from you," Grandma said. "One cannot be only a chestnut, a spendthrift, or a corporate manager, there has to be summer in him as well."

When Boris moved into 'the other woman's' flat, she was a physicist, too, and a colleague. Grandma Dora forbade us to mention her name. "That woman, thank God, is made of chestnuts and lies," the old woman concluded and heaved a deep sigh of relief. Even when the boys fought they did it with the summer I gave them, Grandma thought. On the other hand, she held the walking stick firmly in her hand and knocked down all chestnuts from the trees, muttering under her breath that she felt sorry for me. I was twenty five and she could see how empty-headed I was.

I had two wild kids who could not sit peacefully for a minute, not if their lives depended upon it. Sometimes Boris rang me up. Those were days when chestnut trees blossomed and flocks of swallows came from the South. I thought about my classes. I had already learned that money meant the world, and I had none. I translated one more book with two million explosions and hot sex into Bulgarian. Unfortunately, I also spent every penny I earned in one week. "You should translate Bashevis Singer. He was one of us, and he's no crap like your books," Grandma Dora muttered. "O, your kids are naughty. Look at their clothes. They cut them with pairs and pairs of scissors."

Chestnut trees grew in my sons. Boris was in them, and I could not hate him the way Grandma Dora wanted me to. "He lives with the other woman," she never failed to remind me, but why should I have cared? Boris had given me chestnuts and the sky.

My boys wore out each a pair of trainers a month, and finished the last can of compote in March. Around this time, I began walking to school and Grandma stopped drinking her vodka. Her heart turned into an express train several times a day. And it was only because of she was still on friendly terms with death that the woman remained whole and kicking. "You are not all there," Grandma would say. "That one made you crazy!" At this point she had made up her mind that although she was old like the crags, she had to do something for me, the crazy woman who knew that money was everything, but ran like mad to the chestnut trees. Of course "that one" was never there, but her granddaughter rushed to the chestnut shadows in Radomir, smiling at the sun. Why should she grin idiotically like that after the sun scorched the garden and the old car would not start? Her granddaughter was no good. No good at all.

I was happy under the chestnut trees. The birds that Boris and I had tamed together still lived there. We had tamed the wind, too, and tied it in the grass to get some sleep. "Such a woman should be nuts," Grandma said. One day she announced she had by chance found a tenant for one of the rooms in our two-room flat. All of us: the boys, Grandma and I, flocked together in the other. You could only call it a "room" if your imagination ran wild: four beds, two desks and a TV set—all of them battered—the TV set broadcasting either a yellow or blue tint according to meteorological conditions. If it rained, the screen was blue, if the sun shone, everything was yellow.

The tenant moved into the room we vacated. He was a quiet fellow, very clean indeed, Grandma said. He wouldn't kill a cockroach if he saw one, a meek and mild chemist who worked in the toothpaste factory not far from Radomir. "That guy is great for you," Grandma said directly. She was no good at beating about the bush. "I've been looking for a tenant a year now. I turned down a dozen of them, you know. This one's good for you." The man stammered slightly and when he told me, "Y-y-you are pp-pretty," he blushed furiously up to his eyebrows. Perhaps his blood pressure had reached a point not far from Grandma's express train to death. He gave me a ride in his old Ford truck to my school in Radomir; he repaired the faucet that had been leaking since the dawn of time. Grandma Dora treated him to bean soup and asked him to solve some problems in math for my sons who took advantage of the situation and badgered him into reading them a fairy tale. So docile was he. "He's what you need," Grandma said. "He looks at you as if you were a quiet November day."

I found nothing special about the quiet November days. I went on running to the chestnut trees by the motel, I even took Toncho, that meek and mild fellow, there, but no birds nested under his hands. He could not tie the wind in the grass and let it sleep. Toncho was grass and there was no summer in him. He was a room with four battered beds and an old TV set, which always broadcast blue movies because it rained. My sons, my grandmother and I lived in that room and it was all Toncho had.

Our daughter, Toncho's and mine, was a tractable green-eyed tot. There surely was no summer, winter, spring or autumn in her. There was a warm, well-lit room in that child, and if there was any bird in her, it was still in its egg and had not hatched out. Toncho, however, believed the girl was everything. He took my sons to pick mushrooms and autumn leaves.

"Do you see now what I meant?" Grandma asked me triumphantly. She had again started sipping her vodka just to slow down the express train in her heart.

"That one" had stopped calling me. I no longer taught at the professional school in Radomir. We all moved into a new flat in Pernik, a town where there was not a single chestnut tree. But I went to the birches, telling myself they were chestnut trees. I believed I tied the wind in the grass, and it was summer, and I tamed birds, waiting for Boris to ring me up. I didn't know how things with him were. "For all I know," Grandma said. "He lives well with the other woman. And you are nuts, if you ask me."

I was grateful for the summer, for the birds and winds Boris gave me. I hope he lives happily with her, I said to myself. I hoped like that until the day Grandma cried out, "That one!" I couldn't believe it. "I told him you were not available," Grandma Dora hissed. "Hey, where are you off to? Hey, stop it. Come back. The kids will be back from school. Your husband will be back, too! You are nuts!"

"Boris!" I ran out of the old block of flats. There was not a single birch in the neighborhood. He was walking to the bus-stop, gray like the sidewalk.

After his steps, directly through the asphalt, chestnut trees grew.

About the Author

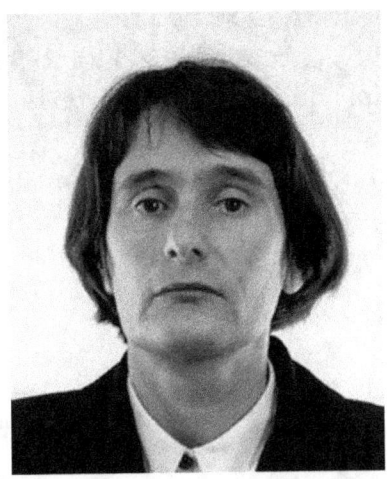

Zdravka Evtimova was born in Bulgaria where she lives and works as literary translator from English, French and German. She has lived and worked as a literary translator in Koeln, Germany and in Brussels, Belgium. Her short stories have appeared in USA, UK, Canada, Australia, Germany, France, Japan, Spain, etc. altogether 21 countries in the world. The following short story collections were published in English: "Bitter Sky", SKREV Press, UK, 2003, "Somebody Else" MAG Press, USA, 2005, "Miss Daniella", SKREV Press, UK 2007, "Good Figure Beautiful Voice, Astemari Publishing, USA, 2008, "Pale and Other Postmodern Bulgarian Stories", Vox Humana, Canada/Israel, 2010. Her novel "God of Traitors" was published by Book for a Buck Publishers, USA 2007. "Vassil" was one of the 15 award winning stories in the BBC world-wide short story competition 2005. In was broadcast by Radio BBC UK in February 2006. "It Is Your Turn" was one of the ten award winning stories, which after a world-wide competition, was included in the anthology "Dix auteurs du monde entire" (Ten Writers from All over the world' In Nantes, France, 2005.

ALL THINGS THAT MATTER PRESS ™

FOR MORE INFORMATION ON TITLES AVAILABLE FROM
ALL THINGS THAT MATTER PRESS, GO TO
http://allthingsthatmatterpress.com
or contact us at
allthingsthatmatterpress@gmail.com